TOMBOY PRINCESS

...AND AN ACCIDENT-PRONE PAPA

PHYLLIS PENDERGRASS

WARNER HOUSE PRESS

Published by Warner House Press of Albertville, Alabama, USA

Tomboy Princess is a fictional memoir. Several names have been changed and the circumstances, exchanges, and conclusions drawn are strictly those of the author and may or may not coincide with the recollections of others.

Chapter 12, "Papa's Back," first appeared online at Moonshine & Magnolias, A Journal for Southern Regional Consciousness, in August 2023.

Warner House Press

1325 Lane Switch Rd.

Albertville, AL 35951

USA

Published 2023

Printed in the USA

27 26 25 24 23 1 2 3 4 5

ISBN: 978-1-951890-52-0 (Pbk), 978-1-951890-53-7 (eBook)

CONTENTS

PREFACE

This book would never have been possible without Papa. He left this world years ago, but his memory lovingly remains with those who knew him. Papa was what some people called a character. Unpredictable—to say the least—and a joy to be around, especially to a precocious little girl who lived in his shadow. Making my childhood magical may not have been his intention, but a goal he accomplished with style and flourish none-the-less.

It is my prayer for memories to be shared, love to flourish, and laughter to abound.

-Phyllis G. Pendergrass

1

A Peddler's Truck

"Do you know something Speck?" He managed to raise his tired old hound dog eyelids long enough to look at me, then let them fall back closed. At least he could tell himself he put in the effort to pay attention when he really just wanted to sleep.

Speck was a black and tan hound with just a "speck," or touch, of white on his nose. He had black, floppy ears that were as soft as velvet, and a black patch of hair on his back that was shaped like a horse's saddle, but the rest of him was reddish-brown. Speck's eyes always looked tired and droopy and a little red around the edges, but he could wake up in a hurry when Mama tossed him some cold cornbread or a homemade biscuit out the kitchen door. He usually scooped up a biscuit before it stopped rolling across the yard.

I loved to sit on the seat of my green swing set and feel the heat of the sun on my back through the thin cotton dress and on the top of my feet. "Mama said my feet are two shades darker than my arms. When I asked her why, do you know what she said? Do you, Speck?" She said, "Why I suppose it must be because your feet are so big. They catch all the tanning the sun has to give." I said, "No, they're just dirty. Then we laughed and laughed. I sure do love Mama, Speck. Just like you love me."

The sun had seemed extra hot before a breeze had started, and I had been twiddling my toes in the loose sand under my swing seat. I loved to feel the heat of the sun on the sand and on the tops of my feet and I could feel the sun on my back through the blue cotton dress I was wearing.

This was my favorite dress of all, and I had worn it so much this summer that it was getting thin across my back, which made it cooler to wear during Alabama's hot summer days. Mostly the dress was light blue, but it had oodles of little white flowers on it too and I liked that. I also liked going barefoot, so the only time I wore shoes was when we went to town, or a funeral.

When I'm swinging, my mind can cover a lot of ground. Right that minute I was watching a bluebird family, where the mama and daddy bird took turns feeding their babies. "I hear them baby bluebirds chirping away in that box over there, Speck. Daddy made that house for those bluebirds so they would have a dry place for their babies. He said when he gets home from work today, I can sit on his shoulders, and he will let me look in the box and see the little ones. He made the top so it would slide open."

Speck didn't care one bit about those bluebirds, he just liked to be petted, so every swing or two I would casually swipe my foot across his back. His fur was so velvety soft and warm from laying in the sun, and it felt ticklish on the bottom of my foot. He was just an old hunting dog who didn't care too much about rabbits or squirrels anymore and hadn't gone possum hunting anytime that I could remember.

"I've known you my whole life Speck, and I reckon I always will. You're my bestest friend in the whole world."

All of a sudden ole Speck raised up his head, cocked it sort of sideways and lifted one ear. If I'd learned anything, it was that hound dogs have good hearing and good noses, so I listened too.

The sound Speck was hearing was the rattle of pots and pans and the sputtering of a tired, worn-out, peddling-truck's motor, dodging potholes on our dusty dirt road. I knew I'd better tell Mama so she wouldn't miss her chance to buy some milk, or eggs, or candy and such.

"Mama! Mama! Mr. Brown is coming! He's topping the hill! Hurry or you might miss him!" I was yelling and running and darting through chickens that scattered in every direction in the yard, all at the same time. Some hens went to the garden, some flew halfway across the yard, and the rooster just stood there in the driveway looking confused. When I had just about made it to the kitchen steps, Mama came out the door.

Daddy and Papa and some other men in the family had built our house themselves. Daddy drew out the plan and Uncle Loy kind of showed everybody what to do. I could still smell the fresh, pine lumber that was used to frame it up.

The house was painted white with shiny new tin on the top and it sat back from the road a little piece with two big oak trees in the front yard. The porch that was on the front of the house was high enough off the ground that I could sit under it and play in the dirt. It was always cooler under the house, and the chickens and Speck enjoyed being under there too. Lots of times we were sitting under there at the same time, usually after lunch when the day was hottest.

"Would you settle down girl? I see him. And now half the neighbors know where he is stopping. You've alerted everyone from here to the next county."

Mama made a swatting motion at my dress-tail as I ran down the driveway, but I was too fast for her and made it to the peddler's truck long before she did.

"Hey, Mr. Brown! How are you today?"

Mr. Brown is sort of short and skinny, with white hair and a scruffy white beard. His blue eyes sparkle when he laughs. Wearing blue denim overalls and usually a white shirt, he drives something that looks like one of the yellow school buses I see parked at the school when we go to town grocery shopping. The side of his truck has a door in it that lifts up and makes a little roof and there is a countertop where he can lay out different candies and other foods people might need. He also sells fabric for making clothes, fishing tackle, and all kinds of useful stuff. I think someday I might drive a peddler truck, like Mr. Brown.

"Well Little One, I'm finer than frog's hair today. It's another beautiful day that our Lord has made. Have you been a good girl for your Mama today?"

"I reckon I have. She hasn't complained anyway, and I haven't gotten any scoldings in a long time."

Mr. Brown laughed and laughed, and it reminded me of a hen cackling. I had just opened my mouth to tell him so when Mama finally got to the end of our driveway. He just stopped in the road and anybody who needed something went to him. If nobody showed up as he drove by real slow, he just went on to the next house.

"Good afternoon, Miss Louise. Are you having a good day today?"

I asked Mama one time why Mr. Brown called her Miss Louise, when everybody else just said Louise. She said it was a sign of respect. I'm going to remember that for when I get old like Mama.

"So far so good, Mr. Brown. So far so good."

"What can I get for you today? I've got some fresh vegetables from local gardens if you need some."

"No, thank you. Our garden has done right well this year. I'll bet I've canned over a hundred quarts of green beans, and I don't know that I'll ever want to eat another bean. Papa said to tell you the watermelons should be ripe next week, if you want to stop by one day and look at them."

"You tell Mr. Orvil that I'll come by Saturday and check with him about the watermelons and I know what you mean about the beans. One time my mother made tater dumplins and my brother bet me I couldn't eat more than he could. He said if I could eat more than him that he would take me fishing. Well,

I dearly loved Mother's tater dumplins and I also loved to fish on the big creek, so the bet was on. I ate so many dumplins that to this day I get a little queasy when I see any kind of dumplin, even apple dumplins, but I sure did enjoy that fishing trip." With his eyes kind of twinkling, he looked at me and winked and laughed.

"Mr. Brown, your poor mother probably has lots of stories to tell about raising you boys. I don't envy her one bit. This one girl keeps me busy enough. I can't imagine having a house full of growing boys to feed and clothe. In fact, she is growing so fast that I need to make her some new dresses before she is out of anything to wear. She grows faster than I can sew, so I need all the head start I can get. Can you show me something for cooler weather?" She looked hopefully into the shadows of the truck.

When the conversation turned to sewing I lost interest. I guessed there wouldn't be any candy for me today, so I said my goodbyes to Mr. Brown and started back to the house.

We had a long driveway that ran between apple trees and honeybee hives. It could get messy in the winter with the heavy rains. The dirt turned to slushy mud and our car would sink almost up to the bottom of the doors. I've seen Daddy leave the car down close to the road so he wouldn't get stuck and just walk to the house, but only during winter and this was definitely not cold weather or the rainy season.

Summer in the south is when the sun shines down so hot that the top of your head blisters through your hair and so do your ears. The rain can stay away for weeks at a time and the dirt driveway gets packed down so much by being driven over that it's nearly as hard as a paved road. By August our pond gets low enough I can walk around the edge in places that's covered by water the rest of the year. Sometimes, if we have dry weather for a long time, the pond gets shallow and the mud in the bottom dries out and cracks. Those cracks are often so wide I can put my hand between them. It makes me feel strange to walk where fish were swimming just a few months earlier.

Mama had told Mr. Brown I needed a new dress for fall of the year. I wasn't too sure when fall was, but I remember her saying school always started when the days got cooler. I was hopeful that hot summer days would stay with us a long time because I got more than a little bit fractious when I thought about having to ride that big ole school bus every day.

Just as I got to the kitchen door Mama came up behind me, grinning like a possum, and held out both her hands.

"Guess which hand?" she asked.

It was a game she played with me sometimes where she would hide a marble or a penny in one of her hands and hold them both out for me to guess which one she had hidden it in.

I tapped her right hand simply because I could see a tiny bit of paper sticking out between two of her fingers. When she opened her fist I saw three Tootsie Rolls and two Laffy Taffys.

"Yippee! Thank you! I love you!" I grabbed the candy, peeled a Tootsie Roll, and popped it into my mouth just as I went through the kitchen door.

"I know you love me. I also know you love Tootsie Rolls." She smiled when she said it. That always made me feel good.

With one jaw filled with the chocolaty treat, I went hunting for my favorite sidekick, my Papa, who was my Daddy's Daddy. Papa lived with us and we went riding together to lots of places in his old blue Ford truck.

He carried me to old covered bridges that had seen better days and we would often fish in their shadows for bass and catfish. He let me tag along when he went looking for wild ginseng and I eventually got fairly tolerable at finding the plants, 'specially if it was the time of the year when the seeds on top of the plants were bright red. Papa would dig up the root, let it dry out, and sell it. He said people used it for medicine when he was a little boy and they still do in some countries like China, wherever that is. I just know it's not anywhere close to my house.

2

FIDDLIN' WORMS

After going into our living room, I settled into a soft, cushy, blue recliner to eat the rest of the candy Mama had given me. That's when I heard Papa puff. He rested his eyes most nearly every day after lunch, by taking off his shoes and socks and stretching out on the couch. Sometimes when he rested, I would sit quietly in the chair close by and watch.

Papa didn't have any teeth. Well, he did have some, but they stayed in a box in his dresser drawer, and he never got them out and wore 'em, so when he laid his head back asleep (I mean resting) his whole mouth seemed to sink in. He would breathe in and out real slow and steady. When he breathed out his lips made a little "puff" sound. I would just laugh, quiet-like, to myself. I got up and eased closer to him.

Now how had I never noticed that? I leaned toward him for a better look. I had gotten within reach of a patch of hair growing out of Papa's ear, had even lifted my arm and formed a pinch out of two fingers. Only a second more and I'd be able to give it a jerk and free it from his ear!

"Gwyn! What do you think you are doing?"

I think I jumped higher than the coffee table!

"Mama! Don't scare me like that! My pigtails went plum over my head!"

When I looked at Mama she was laughing so hard that she was crying. I'd never seen anybody do that before. She was doubled over with her hands on her knees and laughing so loud she had managed to wake Papa up and that meant I'd have to wait about his ear hair. Oh well.

"What are you doing girl? Don't you have anything better to do than wake me up from my eye resting?"

"No, I don't have anything to do. You just missed Mr. Brown stopping by with his peddling truck." I looked at the bare feet that he'd just removed from Mama's couch and couldn't help but notice the bottoms were dirty from working in the fields, but also as thick as the sole of my tennis shoes. I recalled many times seeing him walk barefooted up the chert road in front of our house and never even slowed up or acted like the rocks hurt at all. I was jealous of those feet and hoped someday I'd be able to walk through briers and rocks barefooted too.

Papa always wore overalls, a long-sleeved shirt, and a straw hat. Winter or summer he had on a long sleeve. I never knew how he could stand it in the months of July and August when it was so infernal hot. My toes would get to sweating if I had to wear shoes for too long, much less sleeves.

"What you gonna do now, Papa?" I had high hopes whatever he said would be a fun adventure. Other than Speck, he was my best friend. He lived with us and I figured he always would.

"I was just thinking about fishing. I was wondering if the catfish might be hungry down on Black Creek. I was also wondering where we might find some worms to fish with."

He was scratching the white beard stubble on the side of his face while he spoke. Instead of looking at me, he just cut his eyes in my direction to see how I'd react.

"I'll bet we could fiddle up some worms at Uncle Calvin's woods! I'll bet we could get more than enough!" Oh the excitement at the idea of not only fishing but getting to walk through the woods with a bucket and a handsaw to fiddle for worms. The moment the worms started appearing from around the fiddlin' stump was one of pure joy. The worms were a dark, reddish-brown color and could be almost as long as my arm. Almost.

"We just might do it. Go ask Louise if it's okay for you to go."

I always had to ask Mama if I could go anywhere with Papa, or anyone, but she usually said it was okay. I reckon that was just good manners, to ask and get the okay so she would know where I was. Mamas worried about things like that.

After getting the go-ahead, we started our adventure. First, to get the worms for bait and then away we'd go to Black Creek, because if there's one thing for sure it's that fish won't bite an empty hook. I know, because I've tried.

There are many secret hidey-holes along the creek's banks, where tree limbs hang low along the water's edge. Fishing holes that families pass down for generations, that can't be reached by car, only by walking through overgrown pastures and brier patches. We would go to the closest and easiest to get to today, but sometimes we'd go to another spot called Idell's Pasture and Papa would stop the truck and Miss Idell would come to the door, or out on her tall front porch, and we'd ask permission to go fishing on her place. She always said yes, and usually Papa would give her some watermelons or peas he had grown in his garden.

Miss Idell's property was an adventure, even without fishing. There was a log barn that was even older than Papa, and a cave that had tiny white fish in it and they didn't have any eyes. None of them. I recall wondering how those fish knew how to find food and kept from starving. Daddy said it was a miracle from God and he didn't know the answer. I think he called it a wonderment.

Sitting between that cave and the creek was an old house made out of rough wooden planks that were covered in splinters. There was a porch that went all the way across the front and an old, sagging rocking chair still sitting in the living room, like it still had hopes someone would come back and rock for a while. I wished I could buy Miss Idell's pasture someday and move into that old house. It seemed like that would be a perfectly magical spot.

The best, surest place to fiddle for worms was in Uncle Calvin's woods. Papa would get an old coffee can to put worms in and an old hand saw and away we'd go. Sometimes Uncle Calvin would walk with us to the woods behind his house, but usually it was just me and Papa, and that was alright with me.

To get to the fiddling worms we had to go through some tall grass and around the end of the pond, but first we'd walk by the old barn that was built with big gaps between the planks. I imagined the cow got mighty cold in the winter when the wind blew. Second, we turned right after going by the outhouse and the cherry tree and then on to the pasture fence that I always dreaded having to pass. The fence was barbed wire, but since the cow had gotten out Uncle Calvin had put a strand of electric fence along the inside. It had a double fence!

"Papa, I hate this ole fence. It scares me. I'm afraid the barbed wire will catch my dress and the electric fence will get me when I try to get loose."

I usually crawled under the wire, since I was pretty close to the ground anyway, but Papa just hopped over the top. That fence just always seemed to be waiting to catch me and one time it did. Once I raised up too soon after going under and it burned my behind. I only made that mistake once, because dress or no dress I learned to crawl halfway to the pond before standing up.

"Just because that happened one time doesn't mean it will ever happen again. You learned that lesson and someday before too long you will be tall enough to just step over like I do."

That made me feel a little better and I made it under without problems.

The pasture is covered with a bright yellow flower that is really a weed. I thought it looked pretty, but it was called bitter weed and made a cow's milk taste funny if she ate it. When I spent the night with Uncle Calvin and Aunt Betty, I'd be able to taste it in the milk and the biscuits we had for breakfast. It wasn't bad, just different. Just another something special about my visits.

Through the weeds and tall grass, around the edge of the pond, tippy toe over the rocks at the spillway, walk up the hill on the other side, a sharp left turn into the woods, and the adventure of worm hunting was ready to begin. Not digging for them, but fiddlin' for them. That's what made it extra special, because it seemed that the worms just volunteered to go fishing. Silly worms.

"Always remember when you're hunting a tree to cut it should be about as big as your arm. Not my arm, but your arm. You want it to be small enough to vibrate the ground really good once you start fiddlin'. This one looks about right."

Papa cut the small tree off about knee high. While he was doing that, I was busy finding an old, dead tree limb and used it to rake back the dead leaves that littered the ground around the stump. That was so the worms would be easier to see.

As I cleared a circle around Papa, I could smell the musky, damp dirt under the rotting layer of leaves. I liked the way it smelled, all the odors of the woods seemed wrapped up in it, including leaves and old trees and worms.

As soon as the leaves were out of the way I knew we'd found a good spot to look. The ground was covered with little BB-sized mud balls and that meant that the dirt had been worked up by big, fat, squiggly fishing worms.

Finally, Papa started pulling that handsaw across the top of the small stump, making a crisscross mark and at the same time causing it to vibrate the ground. I could feel it through the bottoms of my bare feet.

"What kind of tree is that, Papa?"

"That was an oak, but it never would have gotten any bigger because these other trees kept the sunlight away from it. To me, oaks do better than some of the other trees. I guess because their roots run down deep into the dirt. They seem to vibrate more, but some people might use a small pine tree. As long as we find worms it really doesn't matter."

After several minutes of feeling the ground vibrating under my feet, I started finding the sticky, squiggly red worms. They weren't exactly slimy, not like a snail is, but gooey from being in that moist wood's dirt. We always added some dirt to the bottom of the bucket so the worms could cover back up. That kept them moist and wiggly until it was time to fish. My fingers felt like they had glue on them when I put the worm on a hook, the kind of glue Mama made for me out of flour except this was icky. The fish sure did love them, sticky, icky goo and all.

Several saw marks across the top of that little oak tree and the ground suddenly seemed to be working alive with the best fishing bait I could ever wish for. Soon we had enough to keep fishing for as long as we wanted, so we picked up our coffee can and hand saw and retraced the way we had come. I could see that confounded electric fence in the distance and already built up a dread to having to avoid it, but when the moment came to go under, I skedaddled under with no problems. What a relief to have that mean ole fence out of the way.

We found Uncle Calvin sitting in the swing under the red-oak trees. Wearing overalls like Papa always wore, and a long-sleeved shirt and baseball cap, he reminded me so much of my Papa. They both bought me surprises when they went to the store. They were brothers, that's what somebody told me anyway.

"We've got more than enough worms for all of us. Why don't you come with us?" Papa always invited him to come along, but he seldom did.

"Wish I could go Orvil, but I got too much to do here today. Don't you and Phillip Glen catch them all and I'll go next time." His blue eyes twinkled when he said it. He'd always called me Phillip Glen even though it's not my name and I'm a girl. It was a name he gave me and only he called me that. Somehow, I think that made me love him even more. Uncle Calvin was like another Papa to me, that's how much I loved him. Today he is wearing overalls with a thin, long-sleeved, green shirt, and a baseball cap. Just like Papa.

"You'll be sorry you didn't come along when we catch everything in Black Creek, maybe even that monster catfish."

Uncle Calvin just let out a big old belly laugh and said, "Now Orvil, we've been fishing that creek for over 60 years and I reckon they'll always be a carp or catfish or two left. Remember when we was little, after Mama died and Daddy was gone off to find work, and we decided it would be a good idea to tie syrup cans to our feet and then go into the creek? We thought we could walk on water like Jesus. We couldn't have been over nine or ten years old."

Papa laughed and said, "Oh, I don't think we was even that old. John was probably twelve and wasn't any smarter than we were. I remember that he wouldn't let us do it until he tried it first. He wanted to make sure it was safe." They both laughed again.

"Well, what happened?" I asked.

"John tied those buckets real good to his ankles and into the creek he jumped. His head went straight towards the muddy creek bottom and the cans kept his feet at the top. He would have drowned right there in that muddy water, with nothing but the bottoms of his feet showing to help people find him, if we hadn't managed to pull him out. We did lots of mighty foolish things when we was young. Of course, we pretty much had to raise ourselves. Wonderment is that we didn't starve. Six kids in ages from just born to 12 years old, just trying not to starve to death."

They both just kind of shook their heads in a sad kind of way. Sounded adventuresome to me, why be sad?

"At least we had Donna to be cooking and trying to steer us in the proper way." That's what Papa said.

Aunt Donna was their older sister and I reckon she was, and always would be, sort of a mother to everybody. I loved to go to her house and sit on the porch in the wooden swing and listen to the grown-ups talk amongst themselves. She always had something cooked, like she knew you would be visiting even before you did.

Finally, I just went and climbed in that old blue Ford pickup, putting the can of worms on the floorboard so I could protect them. It was sort of a sign to say, "Let's get this show on the road." I reckon Papa could read my signs because he got right in the driver's seat and away we went, rattling over that old wooden bridge and hitting every mud hole on that dirt road.

As we rattled and bounced along over the county's rough roads and went around a sharp curve, Papa pointed to an old, falling down, grayish house.

"After I married your grandmother, this is where we set up housekeeping. One night I woke up from a sound sleep and it was so cold I could see my breath. It was winter and we didn't have any way to heat the bedrooms, so they stayed as cold as a freezer. In fact, now that I think of it, at hog killing time we would hang extra meat from the ceiling in the extra bedroom to keep cold and to keep the wild animals from getting to it like they might do if it was outside in the barn, or smokehouse. Well, as I was saying, something woke me up and the first thing I saw was a blue light."

"A blue light? Like the one on Mr. Jim's police car?"

"No, not like that exactly. It was round, and a lighter blue. About the size of the ball you kick around the yard, and it moved around the room. It really just floated in the air, one minute over the bed and then over by the window. Strangest thing I ever did see. Never saw it again and we lived there over five years."

"Did you wake up Grandmother? What did she say?"

"No, I didn't even think about waking her up. I was just so interested in that blue light. There wasn't many cars on the roads then, and if there had been it wouldn't have had any blue lights. Many, many years later I went to a fortune teller and she told me about that light. I didn't even have to ask her about it. She said it was a spirit and if I had talked to it, I would have been shown where to find buried money."

"Wow! Did you look for the treasure?" My eyes felt as big as moon pies. I could just imagine digging for a box full of money and dragging it home for all to see.

"I did look. You bet I did, but I didn't find so much as a nickel. It was probably silly to even look for anything. Whoever heard of a light having buried money?"

"I've never heard of anything like it, but it's sure fun to think about. You can bet I will be thinking about it, Papa. I like that old house, 'specially the porch going around like it does. If I ever build a house it will have a porch that goes all the way around, with shade trees in the front yard and a swing on that porch too. I think I'd paint the house yellow and have a green roof."

I could see that house plain as day in my mind, even the John Deere curtains I'd hang in the kitchen windows. I'd study on that house and someday maybe I could build it. Maybe I could build it at Papa and Grandmother's old home place. That would be nice.

About that time the truck bounced to a stop at the road that ran close to the creek, gravel flying, squirrels scampering up trees, and birds scattering in every direction. To get to the creek from this spot, we would have to walk up the old road that had been closed off, climb over the gate that blocked the road, go through a barbed wire fence, and then scoot down a steep hill on a rocky trail that zigzags all the way to the water's edge.

I took that trail in sections. First, I'd try to get to the pine tree without my feet sliding out from under me. Second, I'd go from the pine tree to the shrub that grew halfway down. Finally, I'd turn loose of the shrub and go the final, and scariest, part of the trail. The last section ended at the creek where a huge oak tree still managed to cling to enough dirt to hold it in place. Whenever I turned loose of that shrub, I aimed for the big oak as a way to stop, and I always gave it a big hug as a way of saying, "Thank you for catching me."

We made it to the bottom of the trail with our fishing poles still in one piece, but sometimes I'd get mine tangled in the briers and bushes that grew at the trail's edge. It was tricky coming down, but it was tiresome for sure trying to get back up to the top. Those chert rocks would roll under my feet, trying to trip me up, no matter how careful I tried to be.

We settled down in our usual spots. I could see the willow trees that leaned over into the water and others that had completely fallen in. On some of the rotting logs that were in the water along the banks, I could see turtles sunning themselves. At the least noise, "plop!" back into the water they'd go and then disappear under the muddy, swirling water. Sometimes the creek was so muddy it looked like milk chocolate, except stinky, and this was the creek Papa told me they use to swim in!"

"Was the water always this muddy? Even when you was little?"

"Yes. It's been muddy anytime I've seen it. Of course, after it rains it's worse because dirt from the surrounding fields washes into it. I don't remember thinking of it as dirty, just muddy. Us boys use to turtle hunt along these banks."

"How do you hunt turtles? The only ones I've seen are on logs and swim away real fast."

"Up under these riverbanks there are holes where the dirt has caved away or maybe something dug them out, I really don't know. The mud turtles would be under the water but backed into those holes and just waiting for a fish to swim by. We use to get in the water and swim along the edge and run our hands along the side of the bank until we felt a hole we thought was big enough for a turtle to get in. Sometimes you'd find a catfish in one of those holes, but we was on the prowl for turtles. Now if we was really hungry, we'd keep the catfish, but a catfish is a scavenger, like a buzzard. They eat what everything else leaves behind. I just never could make myself like catfish."

"When we rammed our arm way back in there and felt the turtle shell, we'd feel across it so we could tell which way its head was pointing. You can tell the front from the back by the ridges on the shell. We caught many a turtle that way. All of us boys were good swimmers."

"But what if you reached in and the turtle was pointed in the wrong direction? Did you ever get bit?"

"I don't recall any of us gettin' bit. I guess it's a good thing because there's an old story that says if a turtle bites you, it won't turn loose until it thunders. Sometimes that might be quite a while. 'Specially in the summer."

"I don't think I'd want to go turtle hunting. Plus, I can't swim."

I just went about my business of putting that slimy, glorious worm on my number eight hook. Sometimes, the worms were so big you had to just hook them in different spots instead of threading them on. The fish liked them either way, but I preferred to thread them on when I could because fish couldn't pull them off as easy. I'd been baiting my own hook since last summer when I went fishing at Uncle Calvin's pond with Daddy. He told me if I was old enough to fish, I was old enough to bait my hook, so that's what I did.

After baiting my hook with a fat, juicy, messy worm, I always cleaned my hands off on my dress. I just couldn't stand the sticky goo the bait left on my hands. Worms weren't my favorite bait, crickets were, but they were nearly impossible to find.

Papa had fixed up two cane fishing poles for us. He said some people call the canes bamboo. He was pretty good at fishing. He tied the fishing line to the cane pole about as far from the end of the pole as my arm is long, then tied it again to the tippy top of the pole. He said that if the end broke off with a big fish you still had it tied to the fishing pole. I thought that was pretty smart. The fishing line was as long as the pole with a fishing hook at the end, a lead weight that is called a sinker above that and sometimes a float above that. Since the line was the same length as the pole, when we quit fishing we could connect the fishing hook to the bottom of the pole and then it wouldn't get in the way. I have seen Uncle Calvin measure the length of string wrong and make it too short, so he would take the tip of his knife blade and bore out a tiny hole at just the right spot to stick that fish hook in, but sometimes it was hard for me to get the hook out that way and I like using the end of the pole better.

The creek bank was tall, and the water was a couple of feet below the top, so when we lowered our lines, they stayed close to the bank. It didn't seem to bother the fish if those juicy worms didn't go too far out into the creek, 'specially the smaller bream. I could usually count on catching several of those. The fun was in not knowing if you might catch a big catfish, bony carp, small bream, a baby turtle, or sometime a crayfish. Papa told me once that a crayfish was a country shrimp. That just made me wonder what a shrimp was. I'd have to ask Daddy. It didn't matter what we caught, because we never kept anything anyway. We always turned them loose, back into the water.

Part of the enjoyment of fishing on the creek was listening to everything around me. The water would make gentle sloshing sounds as it moved along at a slow, casual pace, moving debris downstream so easily and yet forcing rotten logs to bump into fallen trees that had become lodged near the banks. Sometimes, if the current was stronger, the logs floating downstream would turn in circles as they traveled and other times smaller limbs would join in their circle, until they went around the corner and out of sight.

July Flies, or cicadas, would call to each other in the treetops. Their songs would start way up the creek and they'd sing to each other from one tree to the next, until the sound passed over our heads and disappeared downstream. In a minute or two, it would begin again upstream and become almost unbearable as it passed through the treetops, but I always loved hearing it. Their song was part of the joy of fishing on the creek's bank.

Everything was so green and cool, even in the hottest part of summer, or that's how it seemed to me. On the far side of the creek the tree branches reached almost to the water and kept the muddy surface shaded from the hot sun. Fish must have enjoyed those shades because every once in a while, I would see one flop on the surface of the water under those limbs, probably catching bugs that accidentally fell in, or see a turtle pop its head up to get some air before going under and away again.

"Papa, what's around that corner up yonder?"

"I'm not sure girl. It's been a long time since I've wandered up that way. There use to be a sandbar just around the curve. You wanna take a walk up that way?"

"Let's do it! I'm tired of fishing anyway." I'd caught three bream and Papa had caught one carp.

"Look Papa! There's already a trail!"

It wasn't a straight trail but was crooked and so narrow my feet just barely fit comfortably in it to walk. It edged its way along the creek bank, going around the curve in the creek and out of sight.

"The cows made that trail. See how narrow it is? That's because cows place one foot in front of the other when they walk, and I don't reckon they try to walk in a straight line because all cows' trails are crooked as a dog's hind leg."

Papa had taught me to always watch where I was going, 'specially in tall weeds and around water, because you just never knew where a snake might be laying, so as we walked and talked, I made sure to keep my eyes going from one side to the other. Before I knew what was happening, Papa had whipped out his flip with a steel ball-bearing and let it fly. Zing! There was one dead rattlesnake on the trail in front of us. Papa was a bullseye shot with that flip and he just killed a rattlesnake longer than me. I froze to the spot.

"It's okay girl. It's dead. You can come look now."

Sure enough, it was dead. That steel ball had gone plum through that snake's head. One shot equals one dead snake. Just a tree branch in the shape of a Y, two pieces of an old tire's inner tube, and a piece of leather to hold the rock, or in this case a ball-bearing, and a weapon was made. Quieter than a gun and just as dangerous in the right hands.

"Papa! I've never seen a rattlesnake before. It's scary looking. What's that at the end of its tail?"

"That's why they call them "rattle" snakes. Just listen."

He started shaking the tail of the snake and it made such a fuss, like dry rye grass seed when the wind blows, but lots louder. I hadn't heard a thing before he shot it.

"I didn't hear anything. Did it rattle?"

"It rattled just a tad about the time I saw it. If it hadn't been laying in the trail I wouldn't have seen it as soon as I did. That was one lucky shot I made. I'm just glad we're both okay. Do you still want to see what's further upstream?"

"No. I think I'm hungry and ready to go home."

I really wasn't hungry but was having trouble with my tummy feeling icky all at once. Before I knew what he intended to do, Papa had cut those rattles off that snake and put them in his pocket. Then we gathered our fishing stuff and started climbing the steep trail back to the truck, with chert rocks rolling under our feet. I was having second thoughts about grabbing hold of those bushes and trees on the way up, sure there would be another snake just waiting to bite me. I could picture one in my imagination behind every rock and tree.

Once I made it up that hill, under the fence, down the dirt road, over the gate, and inside the truck I felt a whole lot better. That was the biggest snake I had ever seen, and I never wanted to see another one. While I was waiting on Papa to make his way to the truck, I was thinking how glad I was that we didn't have rattlesnakes up on the mountain. We had copperheads and water moccasins, or cottonmouths, but no rattlers. Thank goodness!

"How'd you get so good with a flip? Did you have one when you was a little boy?"

"I don't remember not having one. We all had to hunt for food or we would have starved. Mama died after Ruby was born and sometimes Daddy would leave home for weeks at a time to find work and make money. That just left John and Donna in charge of the rest of us, since they were the oldest. There were times we just about starved, so all of us boys would take to the woods with flips, or fishing poles, or anything else we could find with the hope of finding something to eat. Sometimes one of us might catch some fish, or be lucky enough to knock a squirrel out of a tree using our flip with a rock in it. We would bring it home, skin it, and give it to Donna and she would manage to make a soup out of it so we all lived another day. The next day it all started again. We had it rough, but so did a lot of our neighbors."

"I love Aunt Donna."

"So do I girl. So do I."

3

A Girl And A Flip

"Daddy's home! Daddy's home!"

My feet flew across the soft, tender, green grass in our front yard. Speck was right at my heels, barking at every bounce. My dress-tail was like a kite in the wind and I didn't feel like I even touched the ground, I was just so excited.

"Daddy! Daddy! Look what I've got! Papa made it for me!"

He'd barely had time to turn the car off in the carport before I was at his door, pulling it open. I pushed my latest prized possession into his hand so he could see it better.

"It's a flip Daddy! Papa gave it to me! I'm gonna learn to shoot good with it. He killed a rattlesnake today! It was big but he killed it with one shot. I'm gonna get that good too, then I won't be afraid of anything."

Daddy's eyes shined behind his glasses as he studied the flip. He left early in the morning to go to work at a cotton mill. I was usually asleep when he left, but he always came home a little while after lunch, so I got to see him a long time before bedtime.

He said, "I can tell Daddy made it. He's been making them his whole life, so he's gotten pretty good at it. He told you how to be careful with it? Not to shoot any birds or animals? Don't shoot toward the house or cars?"

"Yes Daddy, and he showed me the best rocks to use. Papa said, not too big and not too small and it needs to be kind of round and smooth. I will be careful. I wouldn't want to hurt a bird or animal anyway, but I would shoot a snake!"

"Well hopefully you will never run up on a snake you have to kill. It never hurts to be prepared, but you be careful."

"Carry me, Daddy?"

"I'll tell you what we'll do. Let's go look in on the baby bluebirds. Maybe they've hatched today."

"They must have because I've seen the Mama and Daddy birds being extra busy today."

As we started across the yard to check on the birds in the little birdhouse Daddy had built, he swung me up on his shoulders for a ride. I knew I had the best, strongest Daddy in the whole world.

When Daddy made the birdhouse, he fixed the top so it would slide over to the side so it could be cleaned out when it needed to be, and so we could look in from time to time and check on whatever eggs or baby birds that might be in there. We had been waiting a long time for these eggs to hatch, and I had been watching the Mama and Daddy birds flying in and out of the box most of the summer.

"Now let's be quiet so we don't scare any bird that might be in there."

I just bobbed my head up and down from my seat on his shoulder as he eased the top back. Leaning over to look as he held me so I wouldn't tip over too far, I could see four sets of little eyes looking back at me. Four cute little blue birds with just one or two fluffy blue-gray feathers and patches of skin the same color. As soon as they saw me they kind of all stuck their necks out and started chirping as loud as they could. Daddy eased the top back in place and we went back to the house.

"They were just so cute! Why did they start such a noise? Because they were scared?"

"I don't think they can really see well enough yet to be scared. Right now when they hear a noise they just think its their mama and daddy bringing their next meal."

"When I grow up I'm going to be a doctor for animals. I love animals, except snakes." A little shiver ran up my arms when I remembered that mean ole rattlesnake.

Sometimes on his way home from work, Daddy stopped at the small community grocery store. Every once in a while he would buy some bucket steak, or cubed steak, and Mama would coat it in flour and salt and fry it in the skillet. When the meat was done, she would make gravy in that same pan that she cooked the meat in. That was some good eating, because not only was the meat and gravy good, but she always fixed a fresh pan of homemade biscuits to go with it. This was one of those days. First, I get to go fishing and then I get a flip. Now we are having steak and gravy and biscuits. It wasn't even Christmas or my birthday!

I stood at the end of our driveway and picked up rocks for my flip. It was still hot although it was late afternoon. Here in the South during the summer months, it was always hot, even at night. Daddy was sitting on the front porch, smoking a cigarette while he had his feet propped up on the rail that runs around the outside of the porch as we waited for Mama to say supper was done.

"Daddy, can I shoot my flip across the road?"

"No. You always shoot back away from the road. Promise?"

"Yes Daddy."

"Supper is done!" Mama yelled from the kitchen door.

"That is music to my ears. How 'bout you, Gwyn? Ready for gravy?"

"You bet I am! Where's Papa?"

Papa lived with us and I knew he wouldn't want to be late to a supper of biscuits and gravy. Mama was the best cook ever, 'specially when it came to biscuits, gravy, and bucket steak. Lots of other things too, but it would take too long to name all my favorites.

"Are you kidding? He was sitting on the couch thirty minutes ago. He's not going to miss a thing when it comes to supper. We better hurry or he might get our share."

That was all I needed to hear to send me running into the kitchen and on into the bathroom to wash my hands. I was ready to dig in!

About the time I got settled into my spot at the table, Papa came in to sit in his seat in front of the kitchen window. He always wore overalls and usually a long-sleeved shirt, no matter how hot it was, and in the summer he went barefooted while working on the farm. I'd seen him walk down the dirt road without shoes on all the way to Uncle Calvin's house, without even slowing up. I wished my feet was as tough as his.

Papa couldn't eat the steak because he didn't have teeth, so he just ate the gravy and biscuits. Well, he did have teeth. I mean, he kept them in a box in his dresser drawer but never put them in his mouth. I'd seen them one time, because he showed them to me and that's when I knew I wasn't ever going to get false teeth!

"Mama, will you sew some pockets on my dresses?"

She looked at me like I had sprouted feathers before she asked, "Now just why, all of a sudden, do you need pockets on your dresses?"

"Well, since I've got this new flip, and I have to keep rocks handy to shoot in the flip, I need somewhere to carry extra rocks. None of my dresses have pockets. I've got to shoot a lot in order to get good like Papa. Isn't that right, Papa?"

"Oh, no. I'm not getting pulled in on this talk. Whatever your Mama says is fine with me." Then he just went on clanging his fork against his plate as he loaded more gravy on a biscuit.

"I might think about sewing pockets on one or two of your older dresses. There's a couple you've about outgrown."

"I love you, Mama. I'm going outside to pet Speck."

Just as the sun set and the frogs started their night-time song, I settled into the porch swing and started rubbing Speck with my foot as I swung back and forth in a slow, lazy rhythm. Instantly, my defender, my trusty friend, the best hound dog in the whole world, was asleep and twitching slightly as he dreamed of chasing rabbits. I spent most of my time swatting at the many mosquitoes that wanted to light on my bare legs. I was about ready to give up the battle and go inside when the front door opened and out stepped Papa.

"Gwyn, since we have those fiddle-worms left I thought we might get some firewood together and go fishing down on the pond tonight. Since we didn't catch anything to brag about on the creek, maybe we might catch one here."

"Can we really? I love fishing at night with a campfire. There's always plenty of dry tree branches around the pond. Can we go now?"

"Now is the best time I know. Get your shoes since you can't see where you'll be stepping."

It didn't take but a second for me to jump my feet inside some old tennis shoes and away we went. I sure would be glad when I was old enough to go fishing all by myself. I'd probably fish every single day.

"Now watch careful when you are picking up branches and make sure it's not a snake. As you know, snakes are crawlin' everywhere. We will fish on this side of the pond where it's clean and there's no high weeds."

There was so many dead tree limbs all over the ground it didn't take but a few minutes before we had a stack tall enough for a fire. Papa was a good fire-starter. I reckon he'd had plenty of practice, with him being so old and all. Many times as we walked across the pasture he would grab a handful of the tall, dry, sagebrush and twist it loose to set the several spots of dry grass on fire. That way he only used one match. He did it all the time.

One time he set a spot of dry weeds on fire and didn't pay attention to where he was standing. In no time at all, one leg of his overalls caught on fire at the hem. Good thing it didn't burn fast and gave him time to notice that the heel of his barefoot was getting hot. He danced a jig around that pasture for a few minutes until he got it put out. Papa keeps me laughing a lot.

If it weren't for the gazillions of mosquitoes, fishing on the pond at night would be perfect. I could hear the fire crackling and popping, feel the warmth on my face and arms, and watch the red-hot embers burn and fall to the bottom of the pile. The wood smoke rose slowly above the flames and I could smell it from where I sat on Daddy's tackle box. There was no breeze, so the smoke just went straight up toward the stars. Our old milk cow would stand on the far side of the fire, just enjoying the warmth and chewing her cud. Crickets chirped in the distance and bull frogs croaked all around the pond's edge. It seemed as though the whole world was at peace and settling down for the night.

Tonight we fished with a rod and reel instead of the cane poles, so I could get the bait way out in the water.

Papa baited my hook with a big, fat, squiggly fiddle-worm, and I cast out as far toward the middle of the pond as I could. I even grunted with the effort, so it would go farther. It was dark, so I couldn't see where the bait landed, but I heard a loud "kerchunk" as it hit the water. Now it was just a matter of waiting for the tug on my line that would tell me to pull in the fish.

"Papa, I don't reckon I remember catching a catfish. Do you? I've seen you catch one at the creek, but I just catch bream and carp."

"I can't say that I do remember you catching one. Maybe tonight will be your lucky night."

"Maybe."

Other than hearing the occasional fish flop on top of the water, all was quiet around the fire, just the usual pond noises could be heard. Buttercup, our yellow cow, stayed in one spot on the far side of the fire, swishing her tail ever so often and belching. Every little bit, she would shift her weight from one foot to the other and Speck, who was laying at my feet, would kick and whine. Papa said Speck must have been dreaming of chasing a rabbit. I hoped he was, because that would be a good dream for a hound dog.

"I'm sleepy. I don't think there's a catfish in this pond."

Papa chuckled and said, "We might as well go to the house, but there's some big ones in here. Once in a while somebody will catch one, usually when they're not trying."

"Okay, let's go. Next time we come fishing let's try not to catch one."

It didn't take but a minute to get our stuff together and put out what remained of the fire. Sleep was waiting on me the minute we got to the house and my head hit the pillow. It had been a good day and I had dreams of catfish as big as wash-tubs swimming around me as I stood waist-deep in water. They swam so close I could reach out my hand and touch them as they swam past. Their whiskers would tickle the palms of my hands with a feather-lite touch. It was a peaceful dream.

4

THE WELL

"What are we going to do today, Papa?"

The sun was shining bright and the day was clear. With a whisper of a breeze stirring, it just seemed like a day made for adventures.

At the kitchen table he finished off the last few drops of his coffee. "Today I'm going to see if I can clean a few rocks from the bottom of the well that's at our old house. It's a good well of water, so I want to take care of it. We've had such a dry summer the water level is down enough I can see what I'm doing."

"How will you do that, Papa?"

"Yes, Papa. How will you do that?" Mama had stopped washing the breakfast dishes, put her hands on her hips, and listened to his plans.

"I'm thinking I can use a rope, tied to our logging tongs, to snag the rocks. Then I'll tie the rope to the back of Ole Blue and pull the rocks right over the top of the well."

"That sounds a tad dangerous. I don't know that I want Gwyn anywhere close while you're working at the well."

"Oh, please! I HAVE to be there! Who will watch after Papa?"

"You do have a point. He does need to be watched."

"Hey! I'm sittin' right here! I hear what you're saying about me."

"Good!" Mama said.

"I don't have to take this abuse!" Papa said with a twinkle in his eye. "Come on, Gwyn. We've got important work to do."

With that he got up from the table, straightened his sweat-stained straw hat, and went out the kitchen door. I was, of course, hot on his heels. This would be something out of the ordinary and I surely didn't want to miss anything.

"What's first?"

"First, I have to find the logging tongs, which I think are hanging on the wall in the corn crib. Second, find that long rope that has been around here longer than you have. Then I'll tie the tongs to the rope and we'll see if we can catch a rock."

Faster than Speck could take a nap, which is pretty fast, Papa had one end of the rope tied to those heavy steel tongs and the other end to the corner of the shiny bumper on the back of his truck. Then we peeped over the wall that circled the well.

The wall was made of rocks, like you find in fields or woods, and came up almost as high as my chin. They were smooth and cool to touch and Papa said the well was lots older than him and had been here as long as anyone could remember. I had to stand on my tippy toes in order to see down to where the water was.

"I don't see any rocks. How do you know where they are?"

"It's like fishing, I reckon. You just toss your line in the water and hope for the best. That's what we're doing."

He picked up the tongs, tied the rope to its two handles, which reminded me of a pair of giant scissors with hooks on each end of the blades, and dropped them straight down into the well.

Kerchunk. The sound echoed off the smooth, rock wall of the well.

"Here we go, Gwyn. Ready or not, I'm pulling it up."

I peered anxiously over the edge, waiting for the hook to clear the top of the water. It took only a few seconds, but I thought that rope had to be a mile long. Finally I could see the metal shining just under the surface, and then it cleared and was in plain view.

"Empty. You didn't get not one thing, Papa."

He didn't say a word, but just tossed the hook and line back into the dark waters of the well. Kerchunk.

He must have pulled that rope up at least a dozen times without anything to show for it, and I'd gotten bored watching him ages ago, but then a miracle happened. He started pulling up the rope, but it wouldn't pull. Could it be? Yes! The moment had come!

"I believe we've got something. It's definitely caught on something that's too heavy for me to lift. You go stand on the porch so you'll be safe and I'll get in the truck and we'll see what we've got."

Papa looped the extra rope around the center of the truck's bumper and into the seat he climbed, ready to do battle with the unseen rock at the bottom of the well.

The motor of the truck started up, blue smoke billowing from the tailpipe, and Papa slid it into gear and gave it the gas. At first nothing happened, just the truck easing forward, but finally the rope tightened. Then tightened some more. Finally, because it was stretched so tight, it looked more like a rubber band than a rope. From my spot on the front porch I could see the moment when those tongs reached the top of the well, but they seemed determined not to go any further, or maybe the rock just didn't want to leave its place in the darkness. For a few precious seconds everything seemed to go still, but Papa had seen the top of the hooks too and was set and determined to finish the job. He pressed the gas and, just as another cloud of blue smoke rolled out, I saw everything in slow motion.

The rope had been banjo string tight anyway and the final push on the gas pedal not only got the tires to spinning but it brought the tongs just a tad further over the top of the well. Next thing I knew I heard a loud 'Kerchunk!' as the rock fell back into the water and I saw several pounds of metal go up into the air, being trailed by a long piece of rope. Up! Up! And into the air over the truck, then down with a loud 'Boom!' and the sound of glass shattering.

"Papa! Papa! Are you okay?" I ran to the truck just as he opened his door, but he didn't get out. He just sat there looking ahead, where a windshield use to be, but now was just scattered all over the inside of the truck. After shattering the windshield, the iron tongs landed on the hood of the truck, where they made a sizable dent and finally came to rest.

"Where's the rock?" Papa wanted to know.

"It fell back into the well and that's when all this happened." I said as I waved my arms in the air.

"Dag-nab-bit! All this for nothing! Well, we'll just have to try again."

"Really? You're going to do this again?" I waved my arms in the air again. It just seemed like the thing to do for some reason.

"Sure I'm going to try again. Look at the truck. I'll be paying out to have it fixed, at least for a new windshield. What are the odds of something like this happening again? I'd say slim to none. Let's go fishing for rocks!"

After another few minutes of dropping the gear and coming up empty, finally Papa said, "I think we have something."

I watched him pull on the line with all his strength, leaning back on the rope. Nothing pulled loose. Maybe this was the one that we could get out today. I sure did hope so.

Now Papa tied the rope to the left side of his back bumper, which was made of a shiny metal. I supposed Papa thought he'd try something different and get better results.

After looping the rope around the bumper several times, Papa hopped into the driver's seat and I went back to my spot on the front porch of the old house. I had a clear view of it all, since the well had been dug in the front yard, between the house and the road.

At first all seemed to be going as I expected. The truck moved forward slowly and the rope became tighter and tighter. The rock didn't seem to be moving up the wall of the well, but I thought it probably would any minute. My eyes were fixed on the top of the well, expecting to see a big rock appear over the rim any time. I could even hear the screech as it moved up the wall and could picture it all so clearly in my mind.

"Wait!" I thought to myself. "Do rocks screech? That didn't sound like a rock."

That's when I noticed the back bumper on Papa's truck. The left corner where the rope was tied was rolling back like a banana peel. Since he was a tad hard-of-hearing, Papa just went right on giving it more gas, until half of that pretty chrome bumper was doubled back towards the middle. Finally, he stopped the truck and got out to see what was taking so long.

"Dag-nab-bit! First the windshield and now the bumper. I reckon the well wins for today. I give up until another time."

"What are you going to do about the bumper? It looks pretty pitiful."

"Oh, that's not a problem. Watch and learn, girl."

I did watch, as he proceeded to drive Ole Blue around the house and toward a big apple tree. Then he backed that truck up beside the tree and tied the bent side of the bumper to the trunk. I couldn't believe what I was seeing when he started backing up, away from that tree. The bumper had straightened out a little. That's when Papa untied the rope and just backed the bumper up against the tree. There was some wrinkles and crinkles in the left side, but that apple tree had at least put everything back in the original position.

After one smashed windshield, one big dent on the truck's hood, and a rear bumper that would always look just a bit droopy, chalk one victory up for the well.

As we walked back into the house, Mama was standing at the kitchen sink, which faced the road. She just had to ask," How did that go? How many rocks did you get out?"

Papa just mumbled and kept on walking through the house and into the living room where he took his shoes off and laid back on the couch for a rest. I figured he needed one, after all he'd done to his truck this morning.

The funny thing is, I was looking at Mama when she asked about this morning's adventures. I'm pretty sure she had a twinkle of laughter lurking just beneath the surface when she said it, 'specially since the kitchen window over the sink faces directly across the road from our old house...and the old well.

5

OVERALLS

Sometimes Papa gets in his truck and goes to the store without me. It doesn't happen very often because I usually manage to catch him before he can get gone, but nobody is perfect. The community store is my favorite. It's just a spot in the road, kind of out to itself with no close neighbors, but it has about anything you could want.

There are two gas pumps in front and as you go in the front door, on the right side is where the ice cream and candy and cold drinks are. On the left side of the store is where they stock some clothes, like men's jeans and coats, and also some tackle boxes, fishing poles and a few toys. This is where Daddy gets the bucket steak too. When some of my cousins come to visit, Papa brings us to get either a cold drink or an ice cream of some kind, then we ride home in the back of his truck while we eat our treats.

Papa drove faster over the dirt roads than he did on the highway. I'm not sure why, but he did. He would always brag to anyone who would listen that his old truck could make it up the mountain in high gear. I guess that was unusual for a truck to do, because people would just kind of shake their head in an amazed way whenever he told them. That mountain has some scary, sharp curves too. One of my cousins was driving up that mountain and Papa was driving down and they met in one of the curves. Papa said their front bumpers kissed, but no damage was done.

I just laughed and laughed and said, "You're so funny! Cars don't kiss!" I don't think Daddy thought it was too funny. I don't recollect him laughing when Papa told it.

Today was one of the times Papa managed to go to the store without me. I was watching Huckleberry Hound and Deputy Dawg on television and didn't hear his truck start up. Now the cartoons were off, so I could hear that old blue truck bouncing over the dirt road, rattling like it would fall apart before making it to the house.

"Mama, Papa's nearly home! What'd he go to the store for? Chewing tobacco?"

"Maybe. Maybe he remembered to get my Dental Snuff."

Mama dipped snuff, Papa chewed tobacco, and Daddy smoked cigarettes. I just liked chocolate and such. Mama's snuff looked like powdered chocolate, but it didn't smell like it. She told me it's ground up tobacco, like what Papa chews. I just think it's all icky. I'd rather have chocolate any day.

As usual, I ran to meet him the minute the truck had stopped. "Papa! Why'd you go to the store without me? You know Mr. Harper likes to see me. Was Mrs. Harper there? Did you re-

member the snuff? What's in the bag? Did you get me something?"

Papa just chuckled a little bit to himself. "Well, I did get the
snuff. Mrs. Harper was there and asked about you. I did get you
something and yes it's in the bag. Does that take care of all your
questions?"

"Oh, a surprise! I was watching cartoons when you left.
Cousin Cliff was on and I do like to watch Deputy Dawg and
Huckleberry Hound. What'd you get me? Can I see it? Can I?"

"Well I reckon you might as well. It's not doing you any good
staying in the bag."

Oh the joy and wonderment when I looked in that bag! I'd
never dreamed of such a thing, but Papa knew I'd love it. That
day was the first day that I wore Liberty Overalls. I couldn't believe my eyes! I'd always worn dresses, had never considered any
other possibilities, but now a whole new world had opened at
my feet. The feeling in my heart at the sight of those brand-new
overalls, a smaller version of the ones worn by Papa, went beyond words! I just threw my arms around Papa, giving him the
biggest hug I could, and made a beeline for Mama.

Mama was waiting on me in the kitchen as I ran through the
door. "Mama! Look what I got! Overalls just like Papa's! Will
you help me put them on?" As I held them up she just shook
her head, but with a grin on her face.

"I can't believe he did it. Girls don't wear pants, much less
overalls. What's next? Cowboy boots and spurs?"

"I don't know, but today it's overalls and will you help me put them on? I want to wear them now."

"Sure. We might as well see if they fit. Let's find you a blouse to wear with them. You can wear them around here and maybe when you go fishing, but not to town. Understand? What will your Daddy say when he gets home?"

As it turned out I don't think he cared one way or another. By the time he got home I had on a red blouse and those dark blue denim overalls and I went struttin' out to meet him. Mama had to roll the cuffs up at the bottom because they were a little too long, but I'm not sure my feet even touched the ground.

As he opened the car door I could see he was laughing and his blue eyes kind of twinkled. "Oh my goodness! What have we here? Are you wearing some of Daddy's clothes?"

"No! These are my very own. Papa got them for me at the store today. I'm going to wear them everyday! Mama says these straps over my shoulders are called gallus? Gallus something? They are what holds the pants up. Do you like them, Daddy?"

"Yes I like them. I think you are the prettiest little tomboy I know."

"What's a tomboy?"

"That's a cute little girl who likes to fish and climb trees."

"I love you Daddy."

"And I love you more Gwyn."

6

CLIMB A MOUNTAIN

Saturday mornings were made for adventures. As soon as my feet hit the floor I made a beeline to find Papa. It didn't take long, because they all still sat at the kitchen table, drinking their last cup of coffee.

Mama said, "Good morning, Gwyn. What are you having for breakfast?"

"Can I have a coffee-soakie biscuit?"

"Yes you can. Coming right up."

Today Mama was wearing a green, cotton dress with little yellow and white flowers all over it. I watched as she added a big slice of homemade butter to the hot biscuit, then sprinkled a big spoonful of sugar over the whole thing and placed it in a shallow bowl.

"Thank you, Mama." I said as she handed me the bowl and a cup of very creamy coffee.

After punching holes in the biscuit with a fork, I slowly added coffee until it was nice and soggy.

"I haven't had a soakie biscuit in a long time. It's yummy."

"Well thank you, dear. You can have one anytime you want it."

Papa stood up at his end of the table, rested his hands by hooking them on the bib of his faded overalls and said, "I thought I might go to the big waterfall in the valley. Does anyone else want to go?

"Me! Me! Me!" I was beyond excited.

Daddy looked over the top of the weekly newspaper and asked Mama, "What do you think, Louise? Are you ready to climb a mountain this morning?"

"Sure I am. What else is there for me to do around here?"

It didn't take but a minute for us to pile into the car and start our adventure. Thirty minutes later we parked at the bottom of the mountain.

Looking toward the top, I could see the waterfall and it was beautymous. (That's the word I use when something is more than just pretty. I heard it on a TV show.) Surely it would take all day to climb that far. Between me and the waterfall were some of the biggest rocks I had ever seen, easily bigger than Papa's old blue truck. Those rocks were scattered all over the woods, with a clear stream of water running down and over and through the middle of them, as it made its way to the small pond at the bottom.

"Daddy, where does all this water go?"

"You see the far side of this pool of water? If you look close you can see a drainage tile that goes from this water, under the road, and then it turns into a stream again and runs downhill until it disappears into Black Creek. Several little streams flow down these mountainsides into that creek, and that helps the creek to not run out of water."

I looked at Papa. "So all the people that live in this valley can water their cows and chickens. Isn't that right, Papa?"

He answered, "Yes. Not only that, but all the wild animals and birds on these mountains and in these valleys can get water too. We wouldn't have any rabbits, squirrels, possums, raccoon, or any other critters if there wasn't enough clean water to go around."

Mama spoke up. "Nothing can grow without water, including trees, grass, or people."

I had never thought of things that way before, that everything is kind of connected.

I was plum bumfuzzled, which means confused according to Papa. My head was spinning, so I looked at everything on the side of the mountain and considered all I'd just been told. I figured I'd give these new ideas some thought when I had some time to myself.

"Mama, where did all these big rocks come from? Have they always been here like this?"

She stopped and looked at all the different-sized rocks that were scattered about the woods, and all the way to the top of the mountain before answering.

"I believe these rocks came from somewhere at the top of this mountain and something happened that caused them to turn loose and roll down to where they are now. Maybe it rained too much, or an earthquake, I'm not sure. Whatever happened, those rocks had nowhere to go but down, and here they sit. Who knows how long they've been there. Maybe even before Papa was born."

"Wow, that's a long time."

We had started making our way up the side of the mountain, with the stream of water on our right side. We sort of zigzagged our way between big rocks and over smaller, moss-covered ones. Many of the larger ones were slanted and stuck sideways, deep into the ground, like a Frisbee. From time to time, I would run up those rocks and look back at the trail we had just traveled. Our car looked like a tiny dot in the distance below.

"Daddy, look at the rocks that are covered by the running water. They have a bright green grass on them."

"Yes they do. It's some kind of moss that loves cool, damp places. You'll see it all through this stream. Close to the pool at the bottom some watercress is growing. It likes to grow near streams too, and it's good to eat."

Just as my legs were getting wobbly and weak from all the climbing, we reached the waterfall. The water came rushing from somewhere over the mountain's top and gushed forward until it fell into a deep rock-lined pool. The water was clear and bubbly and swirled constantly until it began its journey toward Black Creek and beyond.

"Gwyn, hold my hand and we will make our way around the edge and into the space behind the falls." Daddy said, as he reached for my hand.

I never felt afraid when Daddy was with me. As he held my hand and we jumped across a narrow opening between two rocks, I didn't doubt that everything would be fine. When he said we would be safe going behind the waterfall, I followed close in his tracks. Boy, was I glad I did, because seeing the water crashing on the rocks below as we stood behind the veil of mist was something I would never forget.

Daddy said, "Indians use to live behind this waterfall, where it helped keep them warm in winter and cool in summer. These overhanging rocks make a good shelter and would help hold the heat from their campfires. The mist would have cooled the air in the hot summer, and they had water nearby for cooking. Pretty much everything they needed was in this one spot."

Papa, who had been mighty quiet up until now, chimed in. "My grandmother was a Cherokee Indian and lived somewhere in this valley. She told me a story when I was just a young'un about her parents hiding in this area in the 1800's."

"Why did they have to hide, Papa?" I couldn't imagine such a thing.

"The way Granny told it, the government decided that all Indians living in Alabama, Georgia, Florida, and all over this side of the country, had to move to somewhere around Oklahoma to a place fixed for them. They weren't given a choice, just told to get in line and start walking."

"That doesn't seem fair to me."

"It wasn't fair. Some of the land where the Cherokee and Creek Indians lived had gold on it and the government decided to take it. Some of the Indians managed to avoid being caught by the soldiers and hid out in this valley and surrounding hills, which has plenty of caves and water. Thank goodness that Granny's people managed to avoid being captured. They may have hidden behind this very waterfall."

"I'd like to think they did, Papa." Mama said with a few tears in her eyes.

I said, "Me too, Mama. If I ever have to hide just look for me here."

Everybody laughed and we started back down the steep path to our car. It seemed harder to go down than it did climbing up. At one place I sat down on the dirt trail and slid from one tree to another. That seemed safest to me, but I wasn't too sure how Mama would feel when washing day rolled around and she saw the seat of my overalls.

Finally we made it to our car and Mama was so tired she just flopped down, sitting on one of the big rocks closest to the pool of water. She had just relaxed on the surface of that rock when Daddy turned to see where she had gone.

For a second he just looked at her with a funny expression on his face. Then very slowly he said, "Well, Louise. I guess you know you're sitting by a snake."

As soon as the words left his mouth, Mama's hands flew out in front of her, waving in the air. A scream left her throat that sounded like the coyotes we have in the woods close to our house. Similar to a howl, but ear-piercing, and like nothing I had heard before.

Daddy reached out, managed to grab one of her hands and pulled her to her feet. It only took a few seconds from the moment he saw the snake until it was all over, but it was long enough for that snake to disappear in a flurry of leaves from the rock, probably never to be seen again and for sure never working up the nerve to sun itself on a rock.

"What do you mean, letting me sit next to a snake? It could have bit me!"

"I hadn't seen it until you sat next to it. How was I to know that of all the rocks on this mountain, you would decide the one with a snake on it was the one for you?" Then Daddy started laughing, and Papa started laughing, and I started laughing.

Mama stared at us for a minute.

Daddy stopped laughing long enough to say, "It was a water snake and they're not poisonous, so you had nothing to worry about. On the other hand, I doubt that snake will ever be the same after hearing that scream." That's when Mama started laughing too and we all joined in.

Even if I get to be as old as Papa, I'll never forget the sound of Mama's scream as she sat on that rock, and the sight of her hands flapping in the air. I giggled softly to myself as we drove home.

7

Papa Builds a Boat

July sure was hot in Alabama. The wind doesn't blow enough to stir the leaves on our apple trees, and it doesn't rain very much either. The grass in the yard had turned brown and crunched when I walked barefoot across it. There are spots that don't have any grass, just hard-packed dirt. Daddy said by next year we'd have a yard full of grass. I can't help but think it'll sure have to grow a bunch between now and then.

"Papa, when's it 'spose to rain? The yard is brown and the pond is a lot emptier than it was last week. Yesterday, when I went with Daddy to the pond, the water was way down. It was so low at the upper end that the ground was nothing but huge cracks. The mud in the bottom of the pond had dried up and left cracks so big I could put my hand in some of them. It seemed odd to me to put my hand into places the fish use to swim not too long ago. I hope it rains soon."

"We all pray that it rains soon. The garden is as dry as the grass."

Some of my uncles and cousins helped build our house last year. Daddy had made a drawing of what the house should look like and here it stands, with white paint shining in the sun and black shingles on the roof. It has a porch on the front side and the back, big enough for a porch swing. There's also three bedrooms, and an inside bathroom. Our other house stood empty and ignored across the road. It was a good house and sometimes I felt kind of sad when I looked at it and remembered things like the pet skunk that lived under the kitchen. I'd feed it biscuits every morning when it stuck its little black paw up through a knot hole in the floor behind the wood-burning cookstove. That is, until the day I didn't see its little foot searching the plank floor for scraps, and I never saw it again. Mama said it probably went to find a family of its own. Daddy told me that skunks spray a stinky mist all over everything when they get scared. I don't reckon my skunk was ever afraid, because I never smelled anything stinky anywhere, but I missed seeing its little black paw feeling around for a biscuit crust. It was a good skunk.

When he wasn't milking the cow or working in the garden, Papa was building a boat for our pond. It was made of wood and had planks for seats at both ends and one in the middle. I'd just be tickled to try it out and see if fish were easier to catch from a boat than from land.

"Aren't you done yet?"

"Now Gwyn, don't be rushing me. I don't take well to being hurried. We all have our own speed. I still have a few final touches, like sealing the cracks between the planks so it doesn't leak.

If it doesn't rain soon we may not have a pond to put it in. Just a big, dried-up mud waller."

"What happens to the fish if the pond dries up?"

"I guess if it really, truly and completely dried up the fish would die. I'm telling you, I've seen that pond get very low, with the ground at the upper end cracked open and just a little water down at the deep end, but after it rained there was fish in there. Not just baby fish. I mean fish big enough to eat. They must bury down into the mud or something. It's a puzzlement to me."

"How long before the boat's done? Today?" I held my breath and waited for the answer.

"I have to flip it over and seal it with tar and wait for that to dry. A couple of days should do it. Then we'll try it out." He stood up and put his hands on the boat's rim and got ready for the flip.

My Papa is not a big man. He's more like scrawny, short, and apparently not nearly as strong as Daddy, because just as he pulled that boat toward him to turn it bottom-up things started to go wrong.

"Stand back, Gwyn! Don't get too close in case it falls."

Round about then is when the boat reached the place of no return. No returning to its sitting position on its bottom. He couldn't hold it and down the boat came with a big Thump!

"Ouch! D-D-D-Dad-bum-it!" Papa was on the ground rolling around and holding his left foot.

I was kneeling beside him in a heartbeat.

"Papa! Are you okay?"

"No. I'm. Not. Okay. When I pulled on the boat, my feet slid out from under me and under the edge. At least a few of my toes did." Then he kind of rolled around on the ground some more.

"Mama! Mama! Papa's hurt! Mama!"

I could hear him calling to me as I was running full speed toward the house, telling me not to get Mama, but I just wanted her to handle it. She always doctored me when I got hurt. Mama made everything better.

She had been ironing clothes in the back bedroom, but as soon as she heard me yelling she started my way, and met me at the kitchen door. She went out the kitchen door while I was still talking.

Papa had been sitting up until he saw us coming, but then he just fell back onto the grass and groaned a few more times.

"You just beat all. Ben will be home in half an hour and could have helped you lift the boat, but you just couldn't wait. Do you have a grudge against those toes?" Mama was standing with her hands on her hips and she reminded me of one of the superheroes I watched on Saturday morning cartoons. A light breeze gently stirred the sky-blue dress she was wearing, and I could easily picture a red, white, and blue shield covering its front. Mama would make a wonderful superhero.

"I don't need your preaching Louise, just help me stand up and get to the house."

"Oh, I'll help you, it's not like I haven't done it before, and when I get you set down somewhere I'll clean the scrape down your leg and bandage your foot. Lean on me."

"What did you say, Papa? I couldn't hear you." He was mumbling too low for me to understand.

"I said just let me sit in the swing for a minute while you go get what you need for my foot and leg."

I'm not really sure that's what he said. He was looking sort of green around the gills, which means sickly, and had broke out in a sudden sweat. I'm pretty sure Mama wanted to smile for some reason.

The tires on the car had barely stopped turning when I whipped open Daddy's door and started telling him about the day's excitement.

"Guess what happened? Guess what Papa did? You'd never guess! He dropped the boat on his foot!" Suddenly I had his full attention.

"Surely not?"

"Oh yes he did. I was standing right there watching him when it happened. One minute the boat was standing up on its side, and the next 'Bam!' right on his foot! Mama doctored him and he's in the house resting on the couch."

Just before he started through the kitchen door, I remembered something else. "And Daddy?"

"Yes Gwyn?"

"It's the same toes he hurt before." Daddy just nodded his head as he walked into the kitchen, with me following in his shadow.

Mama had done all the doctoring she could for Papa's injuries. She had washed his leg and foot with warm, soapy water, taped his hurting toes together, and covered all the bleeding spots with some stinky salve before wrapping everything in a clean white cloth bandage. She had explained to me that there's really not much you can do for a toe that's broken, except tape it to the ones next to it and hope you don't bump it on anything. Now she was cooking supper and it smelled mighty good.

Daddy had gone on into the living room to check on Papa, but there was nothing for me to see there, so I decided to watch Mama cook. Tonight she was boiling potatoes and peas from the garden and she had fixed something called Cornbread Salad. It had tomatoes, onions, cornbread, and other stuff too. It tasted mighty good to me and sometimes I'd do like Papa and put potato soup over everything. That made all the flavors taste even better.

"I see you saved some plain cornbread for Papa."

"Yes. I thought he'd need a little extra strength since he hurt his foot. He's had a rough day. Would you carry him these two aspirin and sweet tea? I'm sure that foot is hurting a bunch by now. And tell them supper is ready."

I found him relaxing on the couch with his feet propped up on its arm.

"Here you go, Papa. Mama says these should make you feel better, and that supper is done."

"Thank you. Y'all don't wait on me to eat. I'll be there in a minute."

Sure enough, I'd barely started eating when he hobbled his way to the chair at the window and sat down.

"I was just wondering when was the first time you hurt that foot? Can you remember?" I reckon it was about then that Daddy got strangled on a sip of sweet tea.

"Well, the very, very first time I can recall was when I was helping Calvin fix the wheel on an old farm wagon and the pole we used as a lever slipped. That made the axle come down right on my big toe, and of course I was barefoot, which didn't help anything. I was probably about twenty years old. If the rock we'd been using hadn't caught some of the wagon's weight, I guess you'd be calling me Old Flat-Toe."

Daddy spoke up, "Yes, or Old No-Toe. You only get one set you know. It's not like you could grow another toe."

That ended the supper talking for awhile.

8

KICK THE CAN

Daddy says news travels fast where we live, which is out in the country. The closest neighbors we have are most likely family and, if not related by blood, they've lived in the same place so long they've been adopted into the family.

By the time supper dishes had been washed and put away, news about Papa's latest accident had made the rounds in our community. Daddy says the news is helped along by what is called a 'party line' on our phone. That means more than one person uses the same phone line and if I make a call to someone and another person picks up their phone's receiver then that third person can just listen to whatever I say.

Daddy calls our party-line the Rodentown Express because it's so fast. Before sunset, everyone had heard about Papa's latest mishap and several families had come by to visit and get the story retold by the man himself. While the adults sat on the porch, either leaned back against the wall of the house in a straight-backed chair or in the swing, the children decided to play kick the can.

Mama gave us an empty coffee can and we got ready to start. I figured it'd be 'specially fun since it was getting darker every minute, and I'd never played the game before.

"So how do we play this game? I've never heard of it." I had to ask. Being an only child meant I had to wait until my cousins came to visit before playing group games.

"It's easy. You'll love it. Tell her, Mavis," David said. I figured since he was the youngest in the group he didn't know how to play either. Not that he'd ever admit it.

Mavis didn't waste any time before explaining the rules. She said, "It's like Hide and Go Seek. We pick someone to be the Seeker, the one who hunts us after we hide. Then one person takes the can and throws it as far as possible. While the Seeker is running to fetch the can and return it to this spot on the ground, the rest of us run and hide. When the Seeker finds one of us, we both race back to the can. If the one who was found gets to the can first they kick it, or throw it, as far as possible and the Seeker has to go get the can and return it to its place while the other one hides again. If the Seeker gets to the can first then they throw the can and run and hide and then the one who was found becomes the one who looks."

Sounded like fun to me.

"Okay. I'm ready. Come play with us, Aunt Gertie?" I asked.

Aunt Gertie was lots of fun. I loved it when she played games with us and was sure Kick the Can would be fun if she was included. Even though she was just a tad on the chunky side, she could get around faster than somebody might think. Tonight she was wearing blue jeans, a red t-shirt, and tennis shoes, and those clothes were perfect for this game.

"I wouldn't mind playing a round or two." she said, as she got up from the folding chair that rested on our front porch.

"Yippie!" All of us kids knew we were in for a treat, 'specially when she volunteered to be the Seeker.

We all gathered around the can in the front yard and Aunt Gertie picked it up, counted backwards from three and threw it as far as she could. The minute she turned it loose we all scattered, running and looking for a good hiding place.

I ran full speed around the corner of the house and into the shadows beyond the reaches of the yard light, dropped down behind the shrub that had grown there and tried to settle down as far as possible. I was hoping my dark blue dress would look like another shadow.

As I squatted there behind the boxwood, I could hear the sound of feet shuffling past and the occasional whisper as two cousins looked for a better hiding spot. Suddenly, Aunt Gertie came around the corner of the house. I just knew she would find me, but that was the moment Mavis chose to move a little too much from behind the oak tree.

"Aha! I see you," Aunt Gertie yelled out.

The race was on and it was close as they passed the hedge where I was hiding. I stuck my head out as they went around the corner at the back of the house, so I could see better. That was when it happened. I saw it all. Apparently in the excitement of the chase, my aunt forgot about the guy wire that braced our

TV antenna. It was a sturdy, thick wire that ran at an angle from the top of the antenna down to a sturdy metal stob that had been driven into the ground.

Just as Aunt Gertie hit her top speed, her throat hit that wire. Thong! Was the sound I heard and it seemed like our entire house shook. I did say that she was a little on the chunky side and every pound hit that wire at full speed. Poor Auntie was stopped cold and laid out like an old wooden plank, in the pitch black of our back yard.

Being focused on the prize of the can in the front yard, Mavis kept running. She didn't have a clue that her Mama was laying flat on her back and gasping for air a few feet behind her.

"Mama! Mama!" I knew she could fix this because she'd had lots of practice with Papa.

I ran around to the porch in time to hear the grown-ups wondering what the strange noise had been.

"I can't imagine what that was," Papa said.

"I don't know, but I think the house moved. No telling what those kids are doing. And where's Gertie?" Daddy wondered.

"Mama! Daddy! Aunt Gertie ran into the TV wire. It knocked her down and she's not getting up."

They all jumped up and ran around the house behind me. Everyone gathered around about the time Gertie sat up, rubbing her throat and groaning.

"What happened? And why does my throat hurt so bad?"

"Are you okay?" Daddy wanted to know.

"Yes, I'll be okay. I remember now. I was chasing someone and the next thing I knew I was knocked flat on my back. Help me up and I'll be fine. Just no more kicking cans for me tonight. All I want is an aspirin and my bed."

Daddy helped Aunt Gertie up and to her car. She was moving slow and hunched over, but at least she was moving.

"Come on kids. Pile in and let's get home."

Everyone climbed in their faded blue Ford Galaxy and away they went. They even carried the can we used home with them. That's okay, and I understood, because it was an awesome kicking can and Daddy and Papa drank lots of coffee.

9

A BICYCLE AND A POSSUM

The afternoon sun was hot, but the shade of the pecan trees cooled everything down. That's where I liked to play best of all and where Daddy put my swing-set. I had cool, green, grass under my feet here, but I'd have it worn down to bare dirt in no time. Speck would help me.

I was swinging as high as I could and Daddy was sitting in a chair he had made out of scrap pieces of planks. It was painted white and was smooth and cool under my hand when I touched it. Two people could sit in it, but right now it was just Daddy and Speck.

"I like my swing here, Daddy."

He looked up from reading the newspaper and asked, "And what do you like about it being here?"

"It's not so hot here. I can play on the slide and it's not hot on my bottom."

Daddy smiled.

"But best is that you sit with me in your chair."

I could see and hear an old, brown truck rattling down the hill on the dirt road below our pond. It had light and dark brown spots on it. Daddy said the darker areas are rust.

"I see Uncle Bob, Daddy. I think he might be coming here."

Sure enough the truck made a sharp left turn into our driveway and ran right up to the house.

Uncle Bob was what Daddy called a character. I'm not sure what that means exactly, but Daddy usually said it when Uncle Bob's name came up.

Dust flew up into the air and swirled around us when Uncle Bob slammed on his brakes to stop. I ran to meet him and, when I got close enough, he swooped me up into his arms and hugged me tight before setting me back down.

"Have you been behaving yourself young lady?" His blue eyes reminded me of Daddy's when they twinkled.

"Yep. I reckon so."

"But the day is young," Daddy said as he stepped up to the truck. Then he said, "Why aren't you on a tractor somewhere? Don't you have some farming to do?"

Uncle Bob nodded his head, pushed his John Deere cap sideways, and said, "There's always something to do, but this was more important. I've been workin' on a project and finished it this morning, so here I am."

"Well alright then. Let's see this project I've been hearing about."

Uncle Bob reached down into the bed of his truck and lifted up a white and red bicycle.

"It's not pretty, Gwyn, but I reckon it'll work just like every other bicycle. I made it for you out of bits and pieces in my shop. How do you like it?"

"I love it! It's the most prettiest thing I've ever seen."

Uncle Bob said, "I'll get you to sit on it and we'll put the seat so you can reach the pedals and your feet can touch the ground."

"Now I put these little wheels on each side, but just until you get the hang of balancing. They can be taken off real easy."

It didn't take two shakes of a dog's tail, that means pretty quick, until I was sitting proudly on the seat of my first bicycle.

Daddy said, "Try riding down the driveway and I'll walk beside you for a bit."

As I balanced and wobbled and peddled down that bumpy driveway, I figured I was the happiest girl on the mountain. I made it all the way down the driveway and back without falling off.

"How's that?" I beamed at the two of them.

"Great." Both said it at the same time.

"I love it, Uncle Bob. It's the prettiest bicycle in the whole world."

"I'm happy that you like it. You just enjoy it and be careful not to get in the road."

"I'll be extra careful. I promise. Thank you so much." With that said, I gave him one last hug and hopped back on my new toy.

After saying goodbye, Uncle Bob climbed in his truck, start-ed it up, and left out in a cloud of blue smoke going home.

The ground seemed to fly past my feet whenever I rode, 'specially after the training wheels came off. I wore a path around the edge of our yard because I rode every day, around and around. Down the hill to the barn, out to Mama's garden, then back to the house.

The chickens would run and scatter when I first started my riding routine, but soon they didn't even twitch from where they lay in the soft, warm, dirt, fluffing their feathers, getting a sun bath. I guess they figured out I wasn't aiming for them and meant them no harm. Farm chickens are smart that way.

I often rode until Daddy came home from work. Like today, I'd stop when I saw our car top the hill and then start up the driveway. That way I'd be waiting when the car stopped on the carport and Daddy's door opened.

"Daddy! I've missed you." He bent down and gave me a big hug.

"I've missed you too, Gwyn. Daddies always miss their little girls and always love them. I'm glad to be home. Let's go inside and see what Louise has cooked for supper. Are you hungry?"

"I'm always hungry, Daddy. Mama says that's because I'm growing taller every day."

"I think she's right about that. At least the part about you getting taller every day. Let's go see what she's cooked so you can grow some more."

"That sounds good to me. I'm hungry and hearing Mama rattle the pots and pans is making my tummy growl." Daddy was still laughing when we went into the kitchen.

Mama said, "Y'all go wash your hands because supper is done. I've baked a chicken, creamed some potatoes, and opened a quart of green beans. Let's eat while it's hot."

Nobody argued at mealtime and, as usual, Mama's cooking was so amazing nothing had a chance to get cold. I didn't waste any time eating my portion, because I wanted to spend more time outside before bedtime.

"Supper was good. I think I will ride my bicycle a few more circles in the yard before it gets dark."

Mama laughed and said, "I wish I had your energy. I'm doing good to keep the house clean."

She kept the cleanest house on the mountain, so I figured she was telling the truth. I forgot all about it when I sat on the seat of my red bicycle. I thought of Uncle Bob every time I looked at it and remembered how happy he'd looked when he lifted it from the bed of his rusty, brown truck.

It was dusky dark, just before night, when I started around the yard. I'd about reached the pine trees below our house when something white caught my eye. Speck, my best friend and favorite ole hound dog, was laying next to it. I thought I'd best check it out, in case Speck needed my help.

After leaning Ole Red, the bicycle, against a tree, I tippy-toed closer. The pine straw covering the ground made it easy for me to be quiet. I didn't want to wake Speck from his nap, since he was old like Papa and needed his rest. As I got just a tad closer I could see that he had caught himself a possum and had laid it out so he could keep a good watch on it, even while he rested his eyes. Possums were probably the ugliest varmint I'd seen. They have wiry, thin white hair on their body and a tail similar to the big blue gophers I'd catch in the corn crib. Their eyes look sunk back into their head, and they have a long snout, but scariest of all is how they hiss at you. I know because I'd seen them on TV on Sunday nights.

Quiet as I could, I ran to the house to get Papa. Possums, skunks, squirrels and rabbits were things he knew about and this was my first up-close visit with a grown possum, so I had lots of questions.

Going in the kitchen door I started calling him.

"Papa? Papa? Daddy, where's Papa?"

"I believe he's watching Gunsmoke on the TV. What's got you in a fizz?"

"I found a possum and it needs checked out. Speck has it down in the pines."

Daddy said, "We won't bother him and Gunsmoke just yet. First, how about I go with you and see what's going on?"

"Okay."

As we walked across the yard, I told him about my find.

"It's just laying there close to Speck. I looked it over and didn't see it move. Its tongue is hanging out and it looks dead."

Daddy said, "It probably is dead, but if it's just hurt, we will try to help it. When I was growing up back in the woods, without any close neighbors, I doctored a good many animals, mostly dogs who'd gotten into a fight or kicked by a cow."

Speck was still resting his eyes until Daddy walked over to look at the possum. When he heard us, he raised up his tired, old head and opened his droopy, hound dog eyes. It only took one glance for him to decide napping was more important than whatever we were there to do, so he went right back to it.

Daddy gently poked the possum with the tip of his shoe and said, "I don't think it's dead."

Surprised, I answered, "How can that be? Look at it! Laying next to Speck, with its eyes closed and its tongue hanging out and not moving."

Daddy chuckled and said, "Just watch."

As he softly nudged the ugly, white possum with his shoe, I saw it move. Just a little bit, and I had to watch close to see it.

"I saw it move, Daddy. Not much, but it for sure did move. Is it hurt?"

"I don't think so, but we will lay it in the tractor seat so we can watch it and see what it does." He picked it up by its tail, which looked like a big rat's tail, and gently laid it onto the tractor's padded seat. Still no signs it was even breathing. We walked over to the nearby yard swing to see what the possum would do when left alone.

At first there was no moving from the varmint, but after a few minutes its eyes opened. It must have liked what it saw, because that stinker stood up, shook itself off, and waddled its way to the barn. I decided that was one smart possum. Not only did it fool me, but it fooled Speck too, and he knew more about animals than I did. I was sure about that.

"And if you ever hear someone talk about playing possum, you've seen it done for yourself, and by a real possum."

Daddy chuckled all the way back to the house and told Mama and Papa all about it. That night I dreamed of sleeping possums and sleeping dogs.

10

GRANDMOTHER'S TEA CAKES

"Oh, boy! You mean Grandmother is going to stay with us a whole week? When is she coming? Can I sleep with her?"

"Your Daddy will pick her up when he comes home today from work. I don't know about you sleeping with her, we'll have to ask her about that. Papa is going with John on a trip out west to visit some people they haven't seen in a very long time and she'll be with us while he's gone."

"Grandmother doesn't stay with us very often. I like it when she does. She cooks tea cakes and pies."

Running outside to play with Speck, I thought it would never get to be time for Daddy to come home. The mailman had delivered the newspaper, Mama's story on the TV had come on and gone off and still no Daddy and Grandmother.

I ran in the kitchen door to find Mama. She was sitting at the table reading a newspaper. "Is it time? Is it time for Grandmother to be here? How much longer?"

"It shouldn't be too much longer. I'm looking forward to seeing her too. She's my Mama and I don't see her near enough to suit me."

"Why doesn't she just stay with us all the time, like Papa does?"

"I wish she could, but with Papa here we just don't have the room. Besides, she wants to see all of her kids and her brothers and sisters too. She visits everybody."

Papa had left earlier today with Uncle John to travel out west, wherever that is. I couldn't ever remember a time when he wasn't here. I missed him already, even if I was excited about Grandmother's visit.

Finally, after what seemed like days of waiting, I saw our blue car top the hill and turn in our driveway. As soon as it had stopped moving, I opened the door and threw my arms around Grandmother!

"It's been so long since you've been here! I missed you!"

"Well, I've missed you too and what a wonderful welcome. Would you like to carry some of my things into the house? That would be a big help to me."

"Sure! I'll help Daddy."

It didn't take long to move her things into Papa's room and I found her and Mama sitting at the kitchen table talking.

Grandmother kept her white hair cut short, above her shoulders, wore soft cotton dresses that came down past her knees, and black shoes.

"Now don't you worry about a thing, Louise. I will take over milking the cow and help around the house too."

"No, Mama. We didn't ask you to stay for you to work, but if you'd do the milking I'd sure appreciate it. It's not something I've had to do very often and to be honest I sure was dreading it."

"Well just don't you dread it anymore."

"When are you going to cook tea cakes, Grandmother?"

"Now Gwyn, don't you set in to bothering her about tea cakes or anything else."

"Maybe tomorrow. How about that? And you can help me."

"Sounds good to me! I can't wait!"

"Now that you've got that settled, run outside and play so me and Mama can catch up on things."

"Okay. I'm so glad you're here, Grandmother. I'll go find Daddy and see what he's doing."

I could hear mumbling and laughing coming from the kitchen as I slammed the screen door on my way out. I'm pretty sure all kids must love their Mamas. I can't imagine not seeing mine every day.

Daddy was sitting in the swing on the front porch when I found him. He was smoking a cigarette and reading the newspaper and drinking a glass of sweet tea.

"Can we go fishing down on the pond? With Papa gone who knows when I'll get the chance to go if you don't go with me? I wouldn't want to stay long because it's nearly time for supper anyway."

Putting down his empty glass and the newspaper, he said, "I just bought a new fishing rod that I haven't tried out. It's called a fly rod and is a little different than the others we fish with. I reckon now would be a good time to try it out. Go tell Louise we'll be back in time for supper and meet me at the utility room."

I ran through the front door and through the kitchen, just passing along the news without even completely stopping. Mama and Grandmother had started cooking, so I knew I didn't have long to fish.

"Here's your fishing rod and it's already got an artificial worm on it. All you have to do is cast out into the water and reel it in. That's all there is to it. You'll know if you hook a fish."

Wow! Nobody had let me fish with the artificial bait before, but here Daddy was just handing it over. I'm pretty sure my feet didn't touch the ground on the way to the pond. I couldn't wait to try out the new bait.

The fly rod that Daddy had was extra long and had a tiny bait on the end. The bait was light because it had to float on the top of the water, not like mine that sunk the minute it landed. I watched Daddy fish for a while. It was so amazing to me, because he was constantly feeding out line and casting out. The bait would land on the top of the water and he would jiggle the line to make it look alive, then he'd jerk back on the line and the small bait would whip through the air before landing on the surface again.

I didn't realize I had wandered closer to Daddy as he fished, until I felt the whoosh of the wind as bait almost caught at my ear. In fact, for just a second I was pretty sure it had taken part of my ear with it. I skedaddled back to my fishing spot, far away from Daddy and the whipping fishing line.

I'd had enough of the fly fishing, so I concentrated on the new experience of fishing with the artificial worm. It was kind of soft and squishy, but plastic, with a hook run through it to hold the fish until I could pull it out of the water. That was the plan anyway. I put the fishing rod back over my shoulder and just as the tip of the rod got even with my head I let off the brake, and the worm sailed into the middle of the pond. I started reeling it in.

"Crank it faster. You don't want it to drag the bottom of the pond."

"But it doesn't need to go faster than the fish. I want them to catch it!"

Daddy chuckled. I liked to hear him laugh.

"We don't want any slow fish."

I felt a tug on the line. It wasn't a tug like it would be if I hung the hook on a weed. This tug pulled back! I'd caught a fish already!

"Daddy! I've got one! It's a big one, too! Help me get it in!"

"You can do it. You caught it. You bring it in. Just crank slow and steady and anytime you feel any slack in the line you crank it a few more rounds."

I thought I'd never get that fish to shore, but just like Daddy said, I got it in. Slow and steady.

"Look how big Daddy! It's the biggest fish I've ever caught! Take it off for me!"

"Oh, no. You're a big girl. You caught it and you can learn to take it off the hook. Put your thumb in its mouth and hold the bottom jaw. Then use your right hand to get a firm grip on the hook and ease it out so you won't damage the fish. See the hook has a small barb on it? You have to give a little push on that so it won't hang on the lip as you take the hook out. Look there! I knew you could do it! You can do anything you set your mind to do. Never doubt that."

I tossed the fish back into the pond and it swam away. Probably going to tell its family about everything it saw while it was out of the water.

"I did it! I'll do it from now on! Wait until I tell Mama!"

"You can tell her now, because it's supper time and I'm hungry. Someday soon we'll catch a bunch of those bass and have a fish fry. Does that sound good?"

"You bet! Maybe we can do it while Grandmother's here."

"Maybe we can. Let's go."

As we walked through the tall grass back toward the house, our old milk cow started walking alongside. Probably because she knew it wouldn't be long until milking time and that's when she would get some sweet feed and cotton seed to munch on. She was so tame, Daddy sat me up on her back and let me ride until we got to the gate at the edge of the yard.

"See you later, Buttercup. I'll go with Grandmother when she milks tonight."

"We'll see. She doesn't have to do the milking. I can do it."

"I know, Daddy. I heard her tell Mama she would be glad to do it."

"Hmm." That's all Daddy said as we went inside to wash the fish smell off our hands before eating.

"Louise, that was one good supper. I haven't had salmon patties and gravy in a coon's age. You haven't lost your touch cooking biscuits either. You always could make biscuits better than I could."

"I had a good teacher, Mama. Nobody can beat you at cooking and everybody knows that."

"If you'll give me the milk bucket and a washcloth I'll get on to the barn and milk. It's been a while since I've done it, but I don't suppose anything has changed."

"Mama, are you sure you want to do this?"

"Yes, I'm sure, Louise. It's the least I can do to help out. Gwyn can show me around the barn. Can't you?"

"You bet I can, Grandmother! Let's go!"

I opened the barn door that led into the stall Papa used for milking Buttercup. He had built a break, or a kind of chute, that held the cow in place while she ate out of her trough as he milked her. The break was built so she didn't have any extra room to turn around in and he slid a plank in behind her so she had to stay where he put her. I also showed Grandmother where he kept the sweet feed.

"You see this window in the hall of the barn? It doesn't have any glass in it and you can pour the feed into the trough from here. Papa has the stall door closed until he gets her feed ready, then he opens the door that lets her in. She just walks right up to that feed and starts eating and he starts milking. I know because I usually watch from that window and talk to him while he's working."

"I'm glad you've been paying attention. Let's get started."

"Sometimes while Papa is milking I look in here in the crib for baby mice. There's been a time or two this summer I've seen a big, black snake in there. Papa says it's a rat snake and that we don't bother them because they help by eating mice."

"Here Gwyn. Why don't you take the bucket and get the feed? I'll stand here and hold the door for you."

"Okay."

I felt like I was about grown up since she was letting me help her. Not only did she let me get the feed, but I also got to pour it into the trough. After I'd done that we went to the side of the barn and opened the door that went into the stall.

"You're all set, Grandmother. When you open that stall door Buttercup will walk right in and up to her feed. That's when you slide that piece of wood behind her and start milking. That's the way Papa does it and I've watched him bunches."

I backed out, latched the barn door, and went around to watch thru the window at Buttercup's head. I could already hear her munching away on her feed. She sure did love her corn, cotton seed, and mixed sweet feed, and seemed to have a look of happiness on her face every time I saw her eating.

The milking seemed to go as usual from my spot in the hall of the barn. I could hear the milk hitting the inside of the bucket. Squirt. Squirt. Squirt. Squirt. Before long, Grandmother was sliding the bar from behind Buttercup's backside and opened the gate that would let her back into the pasture, but she wasn't ready to go to the pasture. That cow was happy to just wander around the stall of the barn and chew her cud, which is how cows digest their food. It's kinda like they eat the same food more than one time. Papa told me about it once, but I thought it was kind of yucky and tried not to listen too much.

As I peeped through a crack at the barn door, which was still latched on the outside, Grandmother seemed fidgety inside the barn.

"I don't like cows when they are walking close to me. Open the door, Gwyn."

"It's okay. She won't hurt you. She's so calm I even get to ride on her back sometimes."

"I'm sure she's a very nice cow, but I've done the milking and I'm ready to come out now."

Something about the way she was acting struck me as funny. It was funny that she didn't just walk behind the cow and out of the barn thru another stall.

"If you don't open this door the police will come and take you to jail."

Just about that time I looked up the road and here came the police chief's car. He lived just down the road from us, so I figured it was a good time to let her out and go to the house.

By the time we got to the kitchen with the milk, Mama was all set to get it ready to put in the refrigerator.

"Mama, you didn't tell me Grandmother was afraid of cows. She's scared of Buttercup."

"Oh, she can't be afraid of a cow surely. Mama?"

"To be honest, she did make me a bit fractious. I was surprised myself, but it has been several years since I'd milked a cow. Having the chute for her to stand in did make me feel more comfortable."

"Now Ben and I both offered to do the milking. If you was afraid you should have said something. There's no point in you doing something that makes you nervous. Just don't you worry about it anymore."

"Oh, no! I'm not going to let a milk cow get the best of me. Before this week is over me and Buttercup will be best friends."

"Well, if you change your mind, don't you mind telling me. You promise?"

"I promise. Now let's get this milk strained and put in the jugs."

When the milk was brought to the house, it had to be poured through a clean, white cloth that Mama kept for that very thing. It wasn't used for anything else and she had several clean ones that she kept in a cabinet drawer in the kitchen. She would put the cloth across the top of the glass, gallon jug and then pour the milk through. It acted like a screen, to catch any trash that might have accidentally gotten in the milk on the way from the barn to the house.

By the next morning, when the milk was cold, the cream would have risen to the top and could be scooped off. That's what Mama used to make butter. She'd put the cream in a clean, glass bowl and would use a wooden paddle to press out any extra milk. Then, after adding a pinch of salt, she would put it in a butter mold which would press it into either a round shape, or a rectangular shape. The mold was made of wood and was a box with a paddle inside that would push the butter out and onto a plate. Then, the butter was put back in the refrigerator until it was needed.

"Don't forget, Grandmother. You promised we'd make tea cakes tomorrow."

She just laughed and said, "Oh, there's no need for me to worry about remembering, because I'm sure you'll remind me."

"I sure will Grandmother. I'm going to bed now. See you in the morning."

As I drifted off to sleep I could hear the mutterings of Mama and Grandmother as they watched TV and talked about things that had happened years ago. Every so often, I'd hear the deeper rumble of Daddy's voice or a chuckle of laughter when he answered a question. I liked to hear him laugh. It made my heart feel lighter somehow.

The next morning, my eyes popped open earlier than usual. For a second I couldn't figure out what was different, then I remembered Grandmother was visiting, so my feet hit the floor and I was ready for breakfast.

"Louise, will you give me the insulin shot?"

"Now Mama, you know how I am with needles. I just don't believe I can do it. Let Ben do it, since he's here. You don't mind, do you dear?"

"I don't mind, but it's up to Miss Dollie."

"I would appreciate it so much. I get so tired of doing it. I'm suppose to do it before I eat."

"Well then, just put the insulin in the syringe and let's get it done and over with."

She went to the refrigerator and got out a small bottle of clear liquid and pulled just a tiny bit into the syringe. Daddy took it from her and quick as a wink he had put the shot into her arm.

"Why do you have to get a shot, Grandmother?"

"I went to the doctor a couple of months ago and he said I was diabetic, and that too much sugar stays in my blood. This insulin helps the sugar stay where it needs to be. The shot doesn't hurt a lot, but it seems worse if I have to give it to myself. Sometimes it's just nearly more than I can do. I'm always grateful when someone else will help me with it."

'Will it bother you about cooking tea cakes?"

She smiled and said, "No. Not a bit. After breakfast we'll get to cooking."

I thought breakfast would never end, but eventually everyone finished eating and the dishes were washed and put away. Then Grandmother started dragging out a big mixing bowl, cookie sheets, biscuit cutter and the rolling pin. Next she got the flour, sugar, vanilla flavoring and milk out and set everything on the cabinet within easy reach.

While she mixed the ingredients in the bowl, I asked, "How did you learn to cook tea cakes?"

"My Mama taught me when I was a little girl. Just like I'll teach you. Each Mama or Grandmother passes it on down to their children."

I was amazed when she measured out two cups of sugar into the big white bowl, then added the vanilla, followed by fresh, soft butter, two eggs, and a cup of buttermilk. Then she added a pinch of baking soda and mixed in flour until the dough was firm enough to handle.

"If the dough is too thin, all you'll have is a sticky, white mess that's not firm enough to work into cookies. I'll show you how to roll out the dough and you can try your hand at it, if you want to? You'll have to wash your hands first."

"Oh, boy! I'll be right back!"

I ran to the bathroom and washed my hands as fast as I could. I even used soap.

"I'm ready to help! What do I do?"

"You can see that I've sprinkled flour on the counter top. That's to keep the dough from sticking to it. Now I'll put the ball of dough on counter and lightly sprinkle it on top with flour. That's so the rolling pin won't stick to it. Now we'll put a little flour on the rolling pin and we are ready to roll." She chuckled softly when she said that.

The rolling pin was just a solid piece of wood that was about as long as the ruler I used to draw pictures. It was round like a drinking glass so you could roll it over dough and flatten it out, and that's what I did. I flattened out the tea cake dough, with Grandmother's help.

"Good job, Gwyn. I couldn't have done better myself. Now I'm going to take this biscuit cutter and make the separate tea cakes. Sometimes I have to dip it in flour too if the dough doesn't want to turn loose of it, but then I press the cutter down into the dough and out comes one little tea cake ready to bake. Let's see how many I can get out of this dough."

She filled two cookie sheets and then put them in the oven.

"Now in about 15 minutes of them baking at 350 degrees in the oven we will have some warm treats to eat."

"Hurry up oven. I can't wait!"

In no time at all, I was enjoying some hot and delicious tea cakes.

"Aren't you going to eat any Grandmother?"

"No. Since I'm diabetic I can't eat anything sweet. It would make me feel sick and we don't want that. I'll just be happy watching you enjoy them."

"Well, that doesn't seem fair. You should get to eat one too."

"It's okay, dear girl. Maybe I can lose a little weight along the way if I leave off eating anything sweet. My dresses are a bit too snug for my liking anyway. You just enjoy them."

"Oh, I will! For sure!"

And I did.

11

GRANDMOTHER GOES FISHING

Grandmother was visiting while Papa was gone to Texas with his brother, John. She was Mama's Mama and when she stayed with us she baked cookies and cakes and all kinds of goodies. Yesterday we fixed tea cakes, and I thought Daddy was going to eat them all himself, but he left a few for me.

Every day was like a holiday when Grandmother visited, because she loves to cook, and I love to eat. On top of that, she had agreed to go to the pond with me while I fished. I wanted to show her how it was done.

It rained last night, so the ground was kind of mushy, but it would take more than a summer shower to keep me from fishing.

"Thanks for coming with me, Grandmother. Mama won't let me fish by myself."

"That's understandable. Part of being a parent is worrying about your young'uns. You just go on and find your fishing spot and I'm going to put this folding chair under that Catawba tree's shade and watch you drag in all those fish."

I didn't waste any time finding a spot to start fishing, but I had barely set the tackle box down when I heard a commotion coming from around the Catawba tree. I turned just in time to witness what seemed to be Grandmother wrestling her folding chair.

Apparently, the ground was muddy under the shade tree and the fight was to see if Grandmother could stay upright or fall into the squishy, stinky, mud. The worst part of the battle was that it wasn't only mud under that tree. Buttercup, our cow, liked to rest under that shade throughout the day and had left splatterings of her own that became mixed with the mud and water. Grandmother's mistake was in wandering a tad too close to the edge.

She tried to steady herself with the chair, but it only seemed to get in her way. First she wobbled to the left, then tilted to the right, and finally leaned forward, but it looked like her feet moved too slow for her body. As she tilted sharply forward I knew the end was near.

"Be careful, Grandmother!"

I saw it all when she fell, still holding the top of the folding chair that had slid and tripped her. Face first into the mud that wasn't just mud. Being a chunky woman, she settled down into the brown and gray mush so deep that the smells buried under it were all set free. Not only did she look like some kind of burrowing animal when she raised her head up for air, but also smelled like one. It was a sad day, until she raised her head up and I saw that her snow-white hair had somehow managed to avoid the mud, but glasses and every other part wore a brown crust so thick it seemed she had no eyes.

She stood up as she finished wallowing around in the stinky mess, cotton dress plastered into every nook and cranny of her body. She tried to walk forward, but the mud wasn't ready to turn her feet loose. When she tried to free her foot and take a step, the shoe stayed where it was, but her foot pulled free and threw her off-balance once again. When she fell backward, flat on her back, I couldn't hold back any longer. I think I laughed harder than I ever had in my life.

I dropped to my knees, in a dryer part of the pasture, with tears rolling down my face. Finally, I had enough control to hold out my hand to her.

"Here, Grandmother. Let me help you stand up. Take my hand."

Raising her head once again, she swiped her glasses from her face in order to see. That's when I had another laughing fit. She looked like some of those jungle animals we watch on Walt Disney every Sunday night. Her eyes were the only clean spot on her body. Kind of like a reverse raccoon, with pale eyes instead of black, or maybe a skunk since her white hair was shining on top of her head.

"When you get tired of laughing just let me know and maybe you can help me up."

"I'm sorry, but if you could see yourself you'd understand. Maybe Mama will take a picture when you get to the house."

"She'll do no such thing!" Grandmother said, as globs of stinking mud fell around her feet with every step.

I ran ahead and got to the kitchen door first. Opening the door, I called out, "Mama, come see what Grandmother did!"

Mama peeped around the door at the same time Grandmother reached the doorsteps. Her eyes got wide and her mouth dropped open.

She said, "What have you done and how many times did you do it?"

"If you must know, I fell into something and it wasn't mud. I believe twice was the magic number. I just need a hot shower and then we'll start supper."

"Oh, no. I hope you don't think you're walking through my house like that? First we'll have to take the water hose to you and see if we can knock the worst of this off before you track through the house. If you don't mind, just step around back here and I'll get the water hose."

The side of our house paid the price for Grandmother's cleaning by being covered in brown, muddy spots that oozed from about midways of the wall down to the ground. Mama just kind of hit the worst spots and then gave Grandmother a robe to put on in our utility room before going inside for a refreshing shower.

I laughed again as I told Mama all about it, but we quieted down when we heard Grandmother open the bathroom door.

She said, "I do feel like a new woman and smell better too. I'm glad I got cleaned up before Bennie Ray got home. This will be a day to remember."

She was right.

The days with Grandmother flew by. By the end of the week she wasn't afraid of Buttercup anymore, because they had gotten to know each other, but she always sent me into the corn crib for the cow feed. She never did make friends with the mice that lived in the corn. One evening about the time I got to the corn and was filling the bucket, she screamed so loud I dropped the bucket, corn and all, and ran for the door.

"What is it? Why did you scream? Did you see a snake?"

She was dancing, or jumping, or something, in a circle outside the crib door. It kind of looked like the dance Indians do on the cowboy shows on TV that Papa watched.

"It was a mouse! A mouse! And it ran toward me!"

Her short, white hair was bouncing up and down, and so was the empty milk bucket. It was so funny that she was afraid of a mouse! I started laughing so hard that she stopped jumping around and started laughing too.

"I know it's silly for a grown woman to be afraid of something so tiny, but I just am. If they are running away from me it's not so bad, but if they run toward me I just can't stand it!"

I filled the bucket again with feed for the cow and she finished milking. I'm sure I'll always be able to remember her jumping around outside the barn with that milk bucket flapping in the air.

The week had flown by and I was going to miss Grandmother. I wished she lived with us too, like Papa did, but Mama said she had other family members to visit. I don't reckon she had a house of her own, she just visited with her children or other family. That seemed sad to me, but after Grandpa died she couldn't live by herself. Mama said she'd never worked, but I'd seen her work aplenty while she was with us. I sure was looking forward to her coming back.

"Grandmother, I'm going to miss you. You're lots of fun."

Daddy was going to drop her off at her sister's house on his way to work. Her clothes had already been put in the backseat of his car and they were about to leave.

"I love you, Gwyn. I'll miss you too. You go back in and finish your breakfast now and I'll see you soon."

As I turned away from her I noticed a tear had eased from her eye and was rolling down her cheek. Mama was crying too, but I understood. I didn't know what I'd do if I couldn't see my Mama.

12

Papa's Back

"Papa's back! Papa's back! Look, Speck!"

We'd been sitting on a soft, grassy spot in the yard watching honeybees on clover blooms. Daddy had put my swing set under the pecan trees so I'd have a cool place to play. Today he had put a smooth river rock beside me, along with a small hammer. I had been busy trying to crack some pecans to eat. It was a slow go and I figured I'd starve to death if this is all I had to eat. It was a good thing I'd heard Papa's old blue truck rattling over the hill towards home, because I'd managed to hit my fingers several times while I was shelling pecans and I needed to take a break.

Speck was excited too. Maybe he wasn't sure exactly why, but he was howling and barking and running with me toward the house. Chickens scattered, running under the front porch, flying up in trees, disappearing under bushes, and the rooster just stood there wondering what just happened. He wasn't sure which way to look first.

By the time Old Blue had come to a stop, but before the dust cloud had settled, I was opening Papa's door and giving him a big hug.

"You've been gone forever, Papa! What did you see? Where did you go? Did you bring me anything? I missed you!"

"I missed you too, Gwyn. I don't think I ever want to leave Alabama again. I'm not built for long trips and although I've seen some beautiful mountains, Sand Mountain is the prettiest one of all."

"Did you have fun? Tell me something funny that happened."

"Well, one thing does come to mind that I thought was funny. I went to visit my Daddy's brother, his name is Wilbur, and he lives in Texas. It was a big city, bigger than anything we have around here. It's so big they have people who just do one thing. For example, police don't catch dogs, dog catchers don't haul garbage, things like that. One morning I got up and three police cars had parked on the side of the street just down from Uncle Wilbur's house. They had their blue lights going and everything. I was curious about what was going on, so I wandered on down that way. I could see something laying in the road but couldn't tell what it was so I asked another man who had come out to see what was going on."

"Was it a wreck? Was someone hurt?" I asked.

"No, and it was the strangest thing. Do you know what those three police cars had blocked the road to protect people from? Fish!"

"Fish?"

"Fish! Laying on the side of the road, like someone just poured them out there. And if having police there to stand guard wasn't strange enough, do you know what happened next?"

"No, what?"

"They called in a huge tractor with a front-end loader bucket on the front to clean them up. That's what they call their 'Street Department'."

"How many fish was there? Like a truck bed full?"

"No! Maybe a dozen, maybe a few less. It took three cars of policemen, one giant front-end loader, one man to drive it, and one man to shovel the fish into the huge tractor bucket. All to get a few fish off the side of the road."

"That's how they do things in the big city? Maybe they don't see fish enough to even know what they are? Reckon they was afraid of them, Papa?"

"I just won't ever understand why the first person who found them didn't just shovel them into a trash can and save everyone a lot of trouble."

We both just shook our heads kind of slow and started for the house. City people did things different than we did.

"Papa, I've surely missed going on adventures. Daddy works and Mama is afraid to drive so I've been right here since you left. Grandmother did come and stay until this morning, but she doesn't drive either. She milked the cow though. It took her a time or two, but her and Buttercup got an understanding."

Papa scratched his stubble of chin whiskers and said, "I've been thinking of going to Black Creek fishing and I think I'll see if Ruby would like to go with us. She hasn't been on a fishing trip for quite a while."

"Oh, boy! I like Aunt Ruby. She's lots of fun. Is she older than you?"

"No, she's the baby of the family. Our Mama died a few weeks after Ruby's birth, so since Donna was the oldest, she pretty much raised her. Papa would leave us kids at home for weeks at a time when he left to find work and Donna and John would have to take care of the rest of us. Ruby spent the first year of her life sleeping in a dresser drawer. It's a wonder she hadn't died, but Donna pulled her through. Well, Donna and God did."

"I'm glad you're back, Papa."

"Me too, Gwyn. Home looks mighty good. Let's go in and see Louise and Ben."

***

The next day was Saturday, so not only would Aunt Ruby go fishing with us, but Mama and Daddy too. We would all go in Papa's Ole Blue, because that way we could carry the cane fishing poles plus the rod and reels. There was no way those cane poles would fit in the trunk of the car. That's what Daddy said.

"Are we going fiddling for worms this morning, Papa?"

"No, we don't have to because Ruby says she has dug up plenty for all of us to fish with."

"Okay, but I like worm hunting, 'specially walking through the woods, listening to the birds and squirrels in the trees. Except for that mean old electric fence at Uncle Calvin's. Daddy, can I ride in the back of the truck with Papa and Aunt Ruby?"

"Sure. If you'll stay sitting down with your back against the cab of the truck."

"Oh, I've got the truck bed all fixed up special for today."

"What do you mean Papa?"

"Just get up here and look."

He swung me up and over the tailgate of the truck and there, against the cab of the truck, sat an extra truck seat. It was plenty big for two or three people to sit on. This was going to be fun!

"Oh, boy! Let's go!"

"As soon as Louise gets here, we will be ready to ride. Me and you will sit in the back and Ruby can ride up front, if she wants to. Here comes Louise and it looks like she's got a bag full of food for us to eat while we're there."

Mama and Daddy got in the cab of the truck, while I sat with Papa in the back. Daddy turned the key and we started our trip in a puff of blue smoke, courtesy of Ole Blue needing a tune-up. It didn't take but a minute or so to get to Aunt Ruby's house.

"Shake a leg, Sister. We don't have all day."

"Just don't you be trying to rush me. I've only got one speed and it's not fast."

Aunt Ruby put her fishing rod in the bed of the truck, along with her tackle box and a can full of worms she had dug up with her shovel just that morning. That meant they were still fresh, squirmy, and moist.

She wore a yellow cotton dress that had tiny pink and white flowers scattered all over the material. Cotton was about the coolest thing a body could wear during the hot summer months, but underneath her pretty dress, she had on a tan pair of men's pants. I'd never seen anybody do that before, because usually women wore dresses, even if they were fishing or working in the fields. It didn't make no never mind to me, and anyways, I wore overalls so it was kind of the same thing. Sort of, I think.

Papa secured that extra seat so it didn't move around not one little bit, and what an improvement over sitting on the rutted, hot metal of the truck bed. Aunt Ruby rode up front with Mama and Daddy, but me and Papa had the most fun because the wind was whipping around us and keeping us cool. In no time at all we had bounced our way to Black Creek. Let the adventure begin!

"Come here young'un and I'll help you down. Then I'll get our fishing stuff out."

Papa hopped down from that truck even faster than me. Everybody else got out and ready to go at a slower pace.

"I'll carry our fishing poles and your tackle box, Ruby. You just carry the worms and follow us. It's pretty steep from up here on the road and down to the creek and be watchful of the little rocks on the trail. Nobody ever works on this to make it easier to get down."

"Just don't worry about me, Brother. I'm still two years younger than you and haven't forgotten how to fish or walk down to a creek." She picked up her fishing rod and can of worms and down the dirt road we went.

Papa stepped through the barbed wire fence first, as usual, and held a gap open for Mama and Aunt Ruby to slip through. Daddy did the same for me and then brought up cow's tail. That means he was last.

Just as I made it through the fence and straightened back up, I heard a strange noise coming from somewhere in front of me and from behind the big pine tree. I looked around and what to my wonderment did I see? There went Aunt Ruby, headfirst, toes marking a trail into the mountain's rich dirt as she went on her belly down the hill. It was a good thing she'd put on that pair of pants under her dress, or we all would have seen way too much. It was over in just a few seconds, but I was replaying the whole thing inside my head after she finally came to a stop at the bottom of the hill, tangled up in blackberry briers and dead leaves.

For an old woman, she popped up from the ground pretty fast. After pushing her light blue bonnet up and out of her eyes and spitting out several twigs and leaves, she said, "My worms! My worms! Where are my worms?"

I started to giggle at the sight of Aunt Ruby standing there, her bonnet still sideways on her head, after digging a trench down the mountain with her toes, worrying about nothing but her fishing worms. About the time my giggles became out-loud laughing, Daddy nudged me with his elbow and gave a look that let me know this might not be the right time to enjoy a belly laugh at Aunt Ruby's expense. I guess maybe we needed to make sure she was okay first. The laughter just dried up, but it would come back later when I talked to Mama about it. She liked to laugh too.

"Here's the worms, Ruby. Are you sure you're okay? A few more inches and you'd have been swimming in the creek with the fish, but you managed to hold on to that can of worms all the way to the bottom." Papa was trying to hide his smile as he said it but wasn't doing a very good job.

"I'm fine, Orvil. Just go on and laugh because I can see you want to."

"Oh, no! I would never laugh at the clumsiness of my sister."

"I wasn't clumsy! The sun blinded me, and I tripped on a rock. Next thing I know I'm snorting mountain dirt up my nose and blazing a new path down the hill. Now let's fish."

"Yes, dear sister. You lead the way. Then I'll know to pull you from the creek if you fall in."

Aunt Ruby made a funny face at him and started laughing, then we all laughed with her. I reckon that must be how brothers and sisters are with each other.

We all finally found a spot to sit and settled in for fishing.

"Here, Gwyn. I brought an extra rod and reel. You can try and see how you like it."

Usually, I would be using a cane pole. My heart soared as I put that squiggly worm on the hook. I'd send that worm clear across the creek to the shade on the other side. Look out catfish! Here it comes!

I stood up, put the fishing rod over my shoulder, gave it a sling, and waited to watch it plop on the other side. And I waited some more. Where was that worm?

Finally, I looked up. Straight up over my head the worm dangled from its line, hung on the tree limb directly over me. I tugged on the line, but it wouldn't come down.

"Daddy, my line is hung. Will you get it loose?"

After reeling in his line, he came over to help me.

"Now just how in tarnation did you manage to get the hook up there?"

After a sharp tug or two the line came loose from the tree limb. With the worm still on the hook, Daddy handed the rod to me, went back to his spot, and sat down.

I checked the worm to make sure it still wiggled on the hook, put the pole over my shoulder once again and let it fly. "Go little worm." That's what I thought, as I waited for it to hit the water on the far side of the creek.

I waited, but I heard no plop. No kerplunk. Looking up into the thick limbs of the oak tree above me, I cringed inside. After several unsuccessful attempts to untangle the line, I did what had to be done.

"Daddy? Will you get my line down for me?"

"Again?"

Mama said, "Well, you did ask her how she did it the first time. Now you know." She said it with a smile on her face. That made things better and even Daddy grinned.

"I'm going back to using the cane pole. I've been here forever and haven't got to fish yet."

Daddy nodded and said, "I think that's a wonderful idea. There's lots of trees around here that get in the way."

He went back to his spot again, and I got down to serious fishing.

It was peaceful sitting on the creek's bank, listening to the July Flies singing to each other in the trees overhead. Nobody talked much at first. I reckon we all just enjoyed watching the muddy water of Black Creek make its way slowly downstream. Today, the water looked more like chocolate milk than anything else, not only because of the color, but it looked thick too. Some days were like that on the creek, and on days like this, even though the water didn't move fast, it still managed to pick up rotting logs from somewhere upstream and swirl them on their journey farther south.

"Look, Aunt Ruby! There's a turtle on that log way over on the other side. I reckon it's sunning itself for a while. Papa told me he use to go turtle hunting on this creek when he was a little boy. Did you go with them?" I loved to hear stories of when Papa and his brothers and sisters grew up, and I figured Aunt Ruby had some new ones I hadn't heard.

"No, Gwyn. I don't recollect actually going in the water turtle hunting. When I got old enough to tag along after them, I believe my job was to run for help when they did something that got them in trouble, or something dangerous. That's what they told me anyway. I was the youngest in the family, but Orvil and Calvin were the two youngest boys, so we played together and tromped through the woods together. They always took good care of me, but there was a few times I had to run for John or Donna because something happened to them."

"Oh, yes, she spent her time with Calvin and me. All the time, and I do mean all the time." Papa laughed as he said it.

"You wouldn't have changed a thing and you know it." She said.

"Tell me a story, Aunt Ruby. What happened that you had to go get help?"

"I remember one time y'all had managed to sneak off without me, but I knew which way you had gone so I followed. I wasn't but a few minutes behind, but by the time I caught up what a sight I found."

"Now just what story are you fixin' to tell, I wonder. Very seldom did we get into trouble." Papa was laughing when he said it.

"This time I think trouble found you. There was a clearing in the middle of the woods where our old cow would eat grass. In the middle of that clearing was one lonesome, pitiful, little oak tree. It might have measured a foot across, but not very tall because the top had broken out at some point in its life. It was just a short, stubby tree. Well guess what was roosting in that tree, Gwyn?"

"What? A buzzard?"

"Two buzzards, by the names of Calvin and Orvil." She laughed so hard when she said it, she snorted through her nose, which made us all laugh.

"Why was they in a tree?"

"Back when we was young, dogs use to have what they called running fits. It would just come on them real sudden and they'd just start running. I don't know what caused it, but everybody was afraid of it. A shaggy, brown, stray dog had started running in circles around Orvil and Calvin, so they climbed the only tree that was close enough. Apparently, your Papa was the first to start climbing, because he was on top and there was Calvin under him, clinging to the trunk of the tree. Now his feet couldn't have been more than three feet off the ground, and he was butting the bottom of Orvil's feet with the top of his head and saying in the most pitiful voice, 'Go higher! Go higher!' He couldn't go up anymore because that tree was just a tall stump with a few green leaves at the top. I turned around and ran to get John, but I laughed a few times on the way whenever I pictured that dog running in circles at the bottom of that tree and Calvin's feet nearly brushing the top of its head every trip it made around."

"What happened then? When you got back?" I'd never heard of a dog having running fits.

"I didn't go back. I just told John where it was and he went."

"Do you remember, Papa?"

"I sure do. We never wore shoes in the summer so the soles of our feet was fairly raw from hugging that tree for so long, not to mention how tired our arms were. When that dog decided to run away, we was so worn out we slid down the trunk of that tree and rested our backs against it. Just too tired to move."

Aunt Ruby said, "I wonder what made dogs do that? Poor things. We didn't have doctors for dogs where we lived, and didn't have any money to pay one if there had been. It was a full-time job trying to take care of each other."

"That's the truth, Ruby. That's the honest truth. We all grew up trying to take care of each other. We sure didn't have anyone else around to do it. Don't seem like Daddy stayed home much after Mama passed away. I wish you could've known her. Fact is, at barely two when we lost her, I don't remember her either. I only know her through the stories Donna and John told us about her. They've both described her as tall and on the skinny side, soft spoken, and that she worked from daylight to bedtime. She had a hard life but managed to show her love to everyone by a simple touch on the arm or a fast hug as she walked by."

"Well, Brother, at least God blessed us with Donna for a sister and John for a brother, because where would we have been without them?"

"True. John taught me how to fish, and I'm about to show you how it's done."

"Ha!" said Aunt Ruby, and the challenge was on!

Mama didn't care much for fishing. I guess maybe she figured somebody needed clean hands to manage the food. Seemed to me she usually did that job. Like when Daddy built a small campfire to heat hot dogs and marshmallows, Mama was the one to put them on the stick for us to hold over the flames. Everything seems to taste better when you eat it outside, 'specially if you cook it on a campfire.

During a fishing trip was one of the rare times we bought anything from the store to drink. Daddy would stop at Smith's Store and, along with a bag of ice, he would put several Coca-Colas in a big, red, metal cooler. Then Mama would put the food that she had prepared inside too, on top of the ice. Everything inside that box stayed icy-cold all day, and it sure tasted good in the heat of a summer's day.

After a few hours Daddy put the fire out, and Mama packed what little scraps of food we hadn't eaten inside the cooler with the ice. Just as she snapped the lid shut, she asked, "What was the fishing count for the day? Who caught the most?"

Papa spoke up and said, "I caught a soft-shelled turtle and one carp."

"Well, I caught a catfish and two crayfish, so I win. I caught three and you just caught two!" Aunt Ruby answered.

"Oh, no! My catches weighed more than yours, so I win!"

Aunt Ruby, having none of that, put it right back to him by saying, "Nobody said anything about how much anything weighed. It's all about the numbers. The total number caught. I win!"

Mama looked at me, grinned, and said, "I can tell they will be fussing over this for quite a while. If Aunt Ruby wants to ride in the back, then just get up front with your Daddy and me."

"Okay I will. I'm tired anyway."

As it turned out, Papa and Aunt Ruby did ride in the back of the truck on the way home. I was happy riding up front, snuggled between Mama and Daddy. Just before I dozed off to sleep, I could hear the mumbling of a brother and sister argument coming from the bed of the truck, and I smiled to myself.

13

Papa's Never Boring

"I'm bored."

Summer was ending and I felt like I'd done everything there was to do. Mama was cooking tea cakes, her mother's recipe, and I was slumped down into a kitchen chair, resting my head on my arms that were folded on the table's top.

"Why don't you go see how many eggs the hens have laid today? That will help the time pass quicker."

I grabbed the pink straw basket by the handle as I went out the kitchen door and down the steps. It was my Easter basket from last year, but now we use it to hold things like eggs and vegetables. It already had two soft kitchen towels laying in the bottom to cushion the eggs so they wouldn't bump against each other and crack. Nobody wants to eat an egg that has been cracked in the nest. I guess maybe sometimes the hen steps on one or they hit each other and break. Mama feeds those to the dog. Speck sure likes them.

"Come on, Speck. You can go with me to gather eggs." His tired old hound dog eyes looked up hopefully at the sound of the word "eggs." He slowly rose to his feet, gave his reddish-brown and black fur a good shake, and followed me to the barn. I'm sure Speck could run if he had to, but I've never seen him prove it. Daddy says he has one speed and that's low first. That means very slow.

The hen nests were in a row in a side shed of the barn. There was six of them, nailed up all in a neat little row along the inside wall, so no rain or bad weather could get to the hen or the eggs. The lumber used to make the nests was so old it had turned gray over the years. It wasn't new, but it still served its purpose.

Our barn had a hall that ran slap down the middle, from front to back, and had big sheds built off both sides. On the right side of the hall was the corn crib, that's where Papa kept the feed for the cow. Built onto the right side of that was the shed that held the hen nests and some farm equipment, like plows and planters and such.

To the left of the hall was the stall where Papa milked the cow every morning and evening. At the back of the milking shed was another shed that was used when the mama cow had a calf. Papa would put the calf in there while he did his milking, then he'd turn it back in with its mama so it could get its supper.

It was a good barn, with planks that had turned gray after being weathered through years of rain and hot sun, with rusted tin covering the top. Usually, the red Farmall tractor sat in the hall of the barn. The tractor had what Papa said was a tricycle front end and I could see that it did look like a very big tricycle because the rear tires were far apart while the front two wheels where squashed close together.

All was quiet as I got close to the shed. I peeped around the corner to see if any hens were still sitting on the nest, but all was clear. Not all hens like it when you reach under them to collect the eggs and they will peck at you with their beak, but it doesn't usually hurt. It's just their way of saying, "Hey! Can't you see I'm busy?"

Since all the chickens were out in the yard looking for bugs to eat, I went from one nest to the next picking up all the eggs. When I had looked in every possible hiding place, I had collected six eggs for Mama.

"Sorry, Speck. No cracked eggs today for you." He dropped his floppy brown ears even lower than they were already and we started back to the house.

"I found six eggs, Mama."

"Well, that's good. I'll glass those with yesterday's eggs. That way they'll be fresh for a long time."

"What does glassing mean? I know you're not going to keep them in a glass."

"Not exactly. I will take lime that is used for canning pickles and such and mix it with water. When it's mixed really well, I'll put it in a glass gallon jug and put freshly laid eggs down into it. You don't wash the eggs before putting them in the lime, just get them fresh from the nest and put them in the lime water. It sets out at room temperature and the eggs will stay good for months and months without being in the refrigerator. That tradition has been used for a long, long time. Granny taught me that when I was a little girl and I never forgot."

"I'll remember too, Mama."

"Good. You might need to know how to do that someday. It won't be long until your daddy will be home. Why don't we go sit on the front porch until then?"

"Sounds good."

The front porch faced to the east, so in the evening it was a cool place to sit since the sun was behind the house. The big pecan trees in the side yard helped to cool the house too. Right now, several squirrels were busy collecting pecans and burying them all over the yard. Seemed like a lot of useless work to me.

"Mama, why do the squirrels spend all their time burying pecans and acorns? Looks mighty tiring to me."

"Think about it, Gwyn. We freeze vegetables in the summer so we will have something to eat in the winter. It's the same for those squirrels. They know cold weather is coming when food will be hard to find, so while the nuts are laying on the ground for the taking, they gather and bury them so they will always have plenty to eat. When they get hungry, you'll see them hopping around the yard and all of a sudden they'll stop and dig like crazy. Next thing you know, up comes a pecan and they run up a tree and eat it."

"Squirrels are funny. I like to watch them, Mama."

"Yes, they are and I do too. Here comes Papa on the tractor. I reckon he's going to run the cutting harr' over the field where his watermelon patch was."

I sat with Mama in the swing and we watched Papa cut the field in front of the house. Those watermelons sure had been good while they lasted. Papa grew the best watermelons around. The same people came back every summer to get watermelons from him and they would get Pinkeye Purple Hull peas from him every year too. Fact is, he had customers that would place their order for several bushels of peas a year in advance.

Papa went from one end of that old garden to the other. We watched him go back and forth, back and forth. He went from the road close to us to the end far away. Over and over. He had started cutting at the top of the hill and all went well until he made his way to the lower part of the field, which was directly in front of the house. About the time he came to our end of the garden, he raised the cutting harr', locked one tractor wheel, and made a sharp swing of the tractor to start back on the next row. Before I knew what was happening, that harr' had whirled around and hung the mailbox! Pretty as you please the mailbox was swinging free and clear behind the tractor and hung on the harr'. He made it halfway down the row before he noticed something was different.

"Look Mama! Papa took up the mailbox!" I was laughing when I said it.

She had been watching the squirrels until I said that, at one glance she started laughing too. There he sat on the tractor, just looking back at the mailbox where it had been pulled along the row, like he expected it to unhook itself and go back where it belonged.

We laughed so loud that he realized we had seen everything, so he climbed down from the tractor, wrestled the mailbox away from the harr', carried it to its old spot beside the road, and pushed it down into the hole it had just made. It leaned a lot to one side, but he just turned around, stuck his tongue out at us, sat back down on the tractor seat and went on cutting, like nothing had happened.

Mama laughed so hard she cried, but it was a good cry, not a sad one. I'm sure I'll remember the way Papa snagged that mailbox for years and years.

14

TRACTOR ONE, PAPA ZERO

Summer is almost over and the leaves on the trees have just started changing colors and falling on the ground. The entire yard is littered with dry leaves of bright yellows, oranges, and rusty reds. When I walk from the house to the barn, I hear the 'crunch, crunch, crunch' of the leaves with every step, and the yard chickens stirring up a noise as they scratch through piles of leaves looking for bugs or worms.

Today, I'm wearing the overalls Papa had bought for me at the beginning of summer. I remember how Mama turned up a cuff on the legs because they were too long, but now they don't need a cuff and the straps over my shoulders have been let out as much as they can go. I must've grown just a smidge taller the last few months.

The old garden spots have been cut under so they can rest until next year. Mama will plant English peas at the end of February or the beginning of March and the whole gardening process will start all over.

"Speck, you sure will miss me when school starts. I don't know what you'll do all day without me here to keep you busy."

I sat down on the front porch steps and started tearing off small chunks of cold biscuit crusts and tossing them to the chickens that had gathered close. By taking turns throwing one to the left, then the right, then the middle, I gave all the chickens a fair chance. Speck even managed to get a crumb or two every once in a while.

"I do believe you are the laziest dog, Speck, but I love you."

After swallowing the last biscuit crumb, he managed to lick my big toe a time or two. I told myself that meant he loved me, but he probably saw a tiny piece of a biscuit that had rested on my foot.

"I can't believe Mama won't let me wear my overalls to school. I'm sure other girls would be wearing them too, or at least blue jeans. She says that girls only wear dresses to school, but when I get old enough, I'll change that rule, Speck. You just wait and see." He managed to lick my toe again before he flopped over on his side for another short nap.

It seemed like by the time he had flopped over, he was snoring. I wonder if all hound dogs snore. They seem to have kind of long noses that would make snoring easy. I stood up and moved closer to the sound. Strange. While Speck did have his usual raspy breathing, I soon realized that wasn't where the main noise was coming from. It was coming from down toward the barn. Maybe in the hall of the barn? Curiosity got the best of me and I went closer to investigate.

It didn't take long to spot the tractor in the hall of the barn and it was running.

The sound of the motor was being muffled by the thick walls of the barn. Just as I got there, Papa turned the tractor off and I could see he was standing at the back working. He was adjusting the cutting harr', getting it ready to be stored inside the shed off the side of the barn. I could hear the sound of the hammer hitting the metal of the farm equipment as he struck some mud from a disc blade.

Once I saw what he was doing, I sort of veered off to the right side of the barn and decided to visit the fruit trees. If I'm lucky, I might find a few stubborn apples hanging from the higher limbs. That wouldn't be a problem because I can climb any tree that has ever grown. I learned a long time ago to latch my bare feet onto either side of the tree's trunk and just shinny right on up.

Sure enough, close to the top of the tree, two of the prettiest yellow apples I'd ever seen was just waiting for me to come along and pick them, and here I was, ready to shoot up those limbs quick as a cat and rescue them from the tree. I didn't get the chance though, because just when I put my foot against the tree to start my climb, Speck started having a fit.

"Speck! What are you barking at? I don't see not one thing!"

I could hear Papa hitting the metal on the cutting harr' with the hammer and it seemed like he had picked up the pace and was pounding even faster than when we had walked by. Oh, well. Back to my apple picking.

By the time I had climbed onto the lowest limbs, the apples had been shook loose and hit the ground. Ha! That was easy. I hopped from the limb I had perched on and scooped up my prizes on my way back to the barn.

I noticed it was strangely quiet in the hall of the barn. There was no tractor running and no noise from the hammer hitting metal. As I came around the corner of the shed, I could see Papa pulling on the equipment behind the tractor. Maybe. Trying. To. Lift. It?

"What you doing, Papa?" I said with a mouthful of the crispy, sweet apple.

"Gwyn! Go get Louise! I need her help!"

"Why do you need Mama?"

Looking pale, kind of sickly and sort of pitiful, he said, "Please just go get her. Go fast!"

"Okay."

I laid the last apples carefully on the grass, next to the wall of the barn, and whirled around to find Mama. Whatever was wrong seemed to be important to Papa and that was good enough for me.

The kitchen's screen door slammed behind me as I flew through the house calling, "Mama! Mama! Papa needs you! He said to come now!"

I could hear her getting up from the couch where she'd been sitting to watch her story on TV. Daddy said it was a "soap opera," which I didn't understand because they didn't sing and

I didn't see anything about soap when I stopped long enough to watch.

"Where is he?"

"In the hall of the barn, behind the tractor. He said hurry."

Her steps got a little faster after that, as she sort of ran to the barn.

"Papa, what have you done?"

"The cutting harr' has come down on my foot and pinned it underneath the blade. Just start the tractor and raise the equipment."

"You'll have to tell me what to do." She climbed up behind the steering wheel and sat down in the seat.

"Take your left foot and press that pedal down. That's the clutch and you'll have to hold it down while you turn the key. When it starts, pull this red lever back and that will make the lift work."

Mama did what he said and in two shakes of a lamb's tail, which is fast, Papa's foot had been pulled to freedom and he fell back onto the powdery dirt in the hall of the barn.

"Is your foot broke? Take your shoe off and let's see what it looks like. Ben'll be home anytime. He can take you to the doctor."

"I don't know if I can stand the thought of taking that boot off. It might be all that's keeping my toes on. Help me get to the house and then we'll see what the damage looks like. Just help me stand up."

I tried to recall why this all seemed so very familiar to me. When Mama was walking Papa back to the house, it came to me. This reminded me of the time when Papa had dropped the boat on his foot.

"Hey Mama, this reminds me of when the boat fell on his toes! You fixed him up good as new that time."

"I hope it's not any worse than that and we won't know much until we get this boot off his foot."

We had made it to the side-yard where the swing was and Mama said, "Do you want to sit in this swing while we look at the damage or do you want to go inside the house before we try it?"

"I'll just sit here on the swing. It's becoming my favorite place to be doctored."

"Okay. I'll go get the doctoring stuff. Don't you dare stand up until I get back."

That's when Daddy got home from work and parked in the carport. He saw us sitting in the swing and I'm pretty sure he closed his eyes and bowed his head before getting out of the car.

Sitting his lunchbox on the top of the car, he leaned back, crossed his arms, and said, "And what kind of day have y'all had?"

Mama came out the kitchen door about then and said, "I can tell you about Papa's day. He managed to get his foot pinned under the blade of the cutting harr'. Maybe you'd like to do the honor of taking his boot off so I can doctor it?"

As Daddy knelt down on his left knee in front of Papa, he said, "Just explain to me, if you'd be so kind, how anyone gets their foot caught like that? You may be the first person in history capable of such a stunt."

A soft groan came from Papa's direction as the boot came off. I think maybe everybody sort of moaned as we saw his foot. It looked worse than any other hurt I could remember seeing. The line was marked plain, straight across his foot, all the way from below the big toe to the little toe, and the toes had a blue look about them. I'd never seen blue toes before.

"I was working on the cutting harr' getting it ready to put in the shed. There was some mud on the discs I wanted to knock off and that's what I was doing when I thought some of the bolts needed tightening up. To start with, I'd had the lift on the tractor up just a little to make it easier to work. I guess I was studying so hard on what I was doing that I didn't notice my foot had moved under the blade, until the weight was pushing down and I couldn't not notice it. I mean, by then it was too late. I couldn't pull my foot out from under because there was too much pressure and, since the tractor wasn't running, I couldn't raise the lift. That's about all there is to it. That's when Gwyn wandered by and asked what I was doing, and I sent her to get Louise and here we sit. The end."

"I truly never know what I'll find when I get home. I think you've dodged the bullet once again."

"What's that mean, Daddy?"

"It means that he seems to have escaped serious injury and although his toes were blue, the color is starting to come back to them, and I don't think he broke any bones. If you hadn't come along, and then found Louise, we would probably be on our way to the hospital right about now. We will keep a watch on it and see how you feel later. Of course, if you think you need to go to the doctor we will go?"

"Oh, no! I'm in no rush to go. Like you said, we'll give it a little time."

"Oh, my apples!" I'd forgotten the apples I'd put next to the barn's wall when I ran for Mama. I'd climbed the tree for those, so no way I'd leave them for some critter to come along during the night and steal.

It didn't take but a minute to retrieve my snack, but I saw that ants had found the one I'd taken a bite or two out of, so I had to throw that one away. That left only one and I wasted no time in munching down and eating it on the way to the house. One apple should fill me up until supper was ready, which should be pretty soon.

Mama had gone back into the kitchen, and that left Daddy and Papa and Speck at the swing by the time I came back from the barn. After a quick look at the toes on that one bare foot, it seemed like they were pinker than before, but the streak left by the blade would be easy to see for several days.

Daddy was talking to Papa, and his voice was the one he uses with me when he's explaining something.

"If we each have a guardian angel you sure keep yours busy. Just a few more minutes and you would be missing all of your toes and half of that foot. Your angel may be applying for a transfer even as we speak."

"I know and you're right. I should be giving my angel a rest. I think there may be more than one."

Daddy kind of chuckled when Papa said that, and I liked the sound. Daddy didn't laugh much, so a chuckle was as close as it was likely to get.

15

OH, THE SHAME

Summer was almost over. The peas had been picked, and the watermelons gathered. Papa had taught me how to thump a watermelon and be able to tell if it was ripe by the way it sounded. I remember him saying, "Now watch and listen."

He thumped one watermelon and then another. I could tell there was a difference in the sounds.

He said, "Could you hear a difference? The higher pitched one is green, but the lower sounding one is ripe. Another pretty good way to tell is look at the part of the vine close to the melon. See this curl that looks like a pig's tail? If it's brown then it's probably ripe, but thumping is a sure-fired way to tell."

The day had just started to warm up, so I was swinging under the pecan tree. As usual, I was rubbing Speck with my bare foot every time I swung past.

"Speck, you're a good dog."

I noticed his tired-looking face and red-rimmed eyes as he slowly raised his head to look at me. That was his way of telling me, "Yes, I hear you".

"We've had a good summer, haven't we? You've chased a rabbit or two but didn't catch one. I'll bet when you was a young dog you could run circles around those rabbits."

At the sound of the kitchen screen door squeaking, I turned to see who it was. Papa came out and said, "I'm going to Calvin's. Do you want to go?"

"You bet I do!"

I skipped all the way to the truck, with my pigtails making every jump I did. I liked having my hair fixed that way, but I sure didn't know who started calling it 'pig tails.' I'd seen several pig's tails and they were all short and curly, and my hair was nothing like that.

"Are you ready for school to start?" Papa asked.

"Now why'd you have to be reminding me of school? It's no fun at all, not like being here on the farm. I can fish, ride my bicycle, pet Speck, and follow you around when I'm home, but at school it's just teachers and kids."

Papa chuckled and said, "I hate to tell you, but you're a kid too. You've got lots to learn and school is a good place to start. I went to school a few years, so you can too."

We bounced around on the truck seat as Papa hit the biggest holes that road had, and it had a bunch. Sometimes the rear end of Ole Blue would kind of go sideways, and Papa said that was called fishtailing. To me, that was a funny word.

Uncle Calvin and Aunt Betty lived just a short piece over the dirt road from us, so it wasn't but a shake of a lamb's tail until we pulled up at their house. Papa pulled the truck off the road, and along the edge of the woods in front of their house.

I'd never seen a house sit as close to the road as this one. I mean, when you took one step off the doorstep, you would be standing in the road. It was a good thing that this was a dirt road and not many cars traveled it. During the driest part of the Summer, when a car zoomed by their house, dust would rise up in a thick, rolling, layer that soon made its way into every nook and cranny. Aunt Betty was always dusting and cleaning.

"Y'all get out and set a spell."

I hadn't seen anybody outside, so I was a bit surprised when I saw Uncle Calvin sitting in the swing, close to where Papa had parked. He had his legs stretched out along the seat. The swing was attached to a metal bar that was lodged in the forks of two oak trees and had been there as long as I could remember.

"Where's Aunt Betty?"

"Last time I saw her was at the barn. I believe she was going to gather the eggs. I'm sure she'd love for you to help her. "

"Oh, boy, I love gathering eggs. It's like Easter when I hunt for colored eggs."

"Well now, Phillip Glen, you just go right on to the barn. Just don't go in until she says it's okay."

"Okay, I won't."

Uncle Calvin has called me Phillip Glen my whole life, and he's the only one who does. He can't hear real good, so I guess he didn't understand my name when I was born. After all these years I reckon I'm stuck with it, and I'm alright with that, since Uncle Calvin is extra special to me.

It didn't take but a minute until I was standing at the barn's front gate. I could see Aunt Betty in one of the stables, checking the hen nests that were just wooden boxes running along one of the inside walls. She was talking to the hens.

"Now girls, keep up the good work. I expect one egg a day from each one of you. I don't think that's too much to ask in return for all the good food I give you. "

The hens made happy little clucking noises that reminded me of singing as they hunted and scratched in the dirt at Aunt Betty's feet. She sprinkled cracked corn for the girls and backed her way toward the gate that led outside. It just so happened to be the same gate that I had perched on, and she didn't have a clue I was sitting there.

It seemed like she would never make her way over to me, but she did, and I was waiting. Just as she was about to back into my legs, I reached out and touched her shoulder and growled like an angry dog. I hope the chickens needed extra rations of feed, because she screamed so loud and bounced around at my feet so much that by the time she slowed herself down the feed bucket was empty. I reckon the bright side would be a yard full of happy hens.

"Gwyndolyn! You know better than to scare an old woman! I could have had a heart attack and died, in the hall of the barn, covered in chicken feathers or worse."

I almost fell backward off the gate when she started ranting, because I was laughing so hard. Tears ran down my face and I could barely catch my breath.

Aunt Betty's face was a fire-engine red as she continued her preaching while walking to the house, clutching her basket of eggs.

"You'll pay for that little girl. God is watching you."

"Can we go to the orchard and pick some cherries? Please?" I had plastered an innocent look on my face, but she wasn't buying any of it.

"No, we are not going to the orchard, or anywhere. I have to sit down for a few minutes and cool off."

I ran ahead of her, up the wooden steps that led to the back porch, high off the ground. There laid the hose, still dripping water from when she'd sprayed the potted ferns hanging around the edge. Suddenly the hose was in my hand and my fingers twitched. Hands steady, I aimed the hose at Aunt Betty's face.

"You put that down young lady."

I just stood there, not saying a word, thinking of how good those cherries would have tasted. The sprayer never wobbled or wavered from its target. What was that target? Aunt Betty's face, of course.

Moving very slowly, like a cat watching a mouse, she came nearer to the first step. Her climb to the top had begun. That's when she issued her final message.

"Now Gwyn, you better not squirt me. If you do, I'm going to spank your backside. I mean it. I will."

I don't know what made me do it, but the next thing I knew my twitching fingers had tightened down on the sprayer and a strong stream of water hit Aunt Betty dead center of her face. My grip never slacked, and I kept the flow on full force until she fought her way to the top step and wrestled the hose from my hands. Before I could turn and run, she had grabbed my arm, sat down on an old wooden chair, turned me face-down over her knees, and spanked my backside with the palm of her hand. I was shocked. I couldn't believe she had really spanked me.

As soon as she turned me loose, I ran through the house, out the front door, and out to the swing in the woods where Uncle Calvin and Papa still sat.

Papa said, "What's got you all stirred up?"

"I'm ready to go now."

He studied me for a second, then said, "Well if you're ready to go home, I guess I'm ready too. We'll see you later, Calvin."

All I could think about on the way home was that I had messed up, and walking in the kitchen and hearing Mama talking on the phone didn't help anything.

"I'm so sorry about that, Betty. Are you sure you're okay? Well good. I'll talk to you later."

The moment I'd dreaded was here. Mama knew.

She slowly turned from the phone, and I had her full attention. Her brown eyes seemed to shine 'specially bright as she said, "I was talking to your Aunt Betty. It seems that she got a shower on her back porch. What would you like to tell me about that?"

That's all it took for me to start crying. I don't mean just a few tears running down my face, but a full-out, wide open crying fit. I ran to the couch, face-down, and through tears, and sobs, and plenty of sniffling, I confessed it all to Mama. She knew it anyway.

"First, I scared Aunt Betty in the barn. Then she wouldn't go to the cherry tree with me. The water hose was just laying there on the porch and I just couldn't seem to put it down after I had picked it up." I cried another few minutes as Mama waited. "Now I can't ever go to Aunt Betty's again."

Mama had been standing beside me while I was talking, but when I finished, she sat on the coffee table and rubbed my back as she spoke.

"Oh, I'm pretty sure you'll go back."

"Really, Mama?" I lifted my head from the couch cushion, wondering if she knew a magical answer to my problem. "You believe I might go back someday?"

"Oh, yes, because we're going back right now so you can apologize to her."

"No Mama! Please don't make me go!" And the tears started again.

The ride didn't take long. Mama drove Papa's Ole Blue and here we sat, once again parked under the shade trees across the road from the house.

"Let's go in," Mama said, as she opened her door and got out.

I dropped my head and pushed my door open, too.

Dragging my feet and kicking at chert rocks, I tried to take as long as possible before I had to face Aunt Betty and apologize.

As soon as we stepped onto the front porch, Uncle Calvin opened the door.

With a grin on his face and a twinkle in his blue eyes, he said, "Y'all come on in and have a seat." He winked at me as I stepped inside. That made the task ahead seem a little easier for some reason.

Aunt Betty was sitting on the couch, and as soon as I got through the door, she held her arms wide open, inviting me over for a big hug. I ran a few steps and was soon wrapped in her arms.

My world suddenly felt lighter and brighter as I asked her to forgive me.

"I'm so sorry. I don't know why I did it, but I'll never do it again. I promise."

After giving another quick hug, she turned me to face her and said, "Now you remember what I'm going to say." She waited until I looked straight into her eyes, then said, "I love you. Nothing will ever change that. We all do things we have to ask forgiveness for from time to time, but I love you and I forgive you and now we won't worry about it anymore. Okay?"

I threw my arms around my favorite aunt one last time and hugged her as hard as I could.

"I love you too, and you too, Uncle Calvin."

His face turned pink as I said it and I'm sure there was a tear that rolled down his cheek. He stood up from the rocking chair and said, "Come on, Phillip Glen. I reckon we've got time to fish a minute or two."

"Yippee!"

Another adventure begins, only this time it's with my favorite uncle.

16

THE DREADED SCHOOL BUS

The kitchen door squeaked and Mama walked onto the top step.

"Come and get your shoes on, and a dress."

I groaned at the idea.

"Why do I need shoes? Do I have to put on a dress?"

"You know school starts today, and yes you'll be wearing a dress."

"Why don't girls get to wear pants or overalls? Miss Sue wears overalls when she plows her garden."

"We're not going to the garden, and when you're old enough to plow with a mule you can wear overalls too."

Dragging myself slowly from the swing, I went into the house and put on my favorite light blue dress and cleanest tennis shoes, hoping that at least I could get away with having comfortable feet. My feet had mostly been free of shoes through the summer, since the only time I had to get dressed up was to go to town or a funeral.

"And brush your hair. Front AND back, please."

I wondered if this punishment would ever end.

I'd had breakfast before going outside, so once I'd put on what Mama considered to be proper clothes, I went back out to sit in the swing and wait on the dreaded school bus. Where had the summer gone?

Our old black and tan hound dog, Speck, flopped down at my feet and made me wonder if he was tired, old, or just wanted petting.

"I hate to tell you, Speck, but this is the first day of school. I'll be gone all day, so I guess you'll have to take care of Papa."

One tired, bloodshot eye opened enough from his place on the ground as if to say, "You think I'm going to lose nap time just to follow at Papa's heels? Dream on, little girl."

The first few days of school were just plum nerve rackin'. Not knowing where to go or when to go, or what if I needed to go. I 'specially dreaded riding the school bus.

I 'spose being an only child, and happy about it, didn't help me get use to people, 'specially kids. I reckon school buses were full of kids who were loud, pushy, and mean and couldn't just sit in the seat and think about the punishment we were all being forced to share. School.

I could still fish after school, but I'd miss seeing Papa in action when he got on the tractor. He could just wait until I was home to go on adventures. I wouldn't be home to see any porcupines or possums, or other varmints, that might wander by while I was off learning stuff. Not much I could do about that.

The minutes ticked slowly by as I sat in that white yard swing, petting Speck every once in a while, as I swung back and forth. Suddenly I saw Speck's ear twitch. That let me know the school bus would be coming over the hill to our house any minute.

I sighed and stood up.

The sun's rays flashed on the orangey-yellow bus as it topped the hill, and I started counting off the minutes until it brought me back home. It came to a screeching halt, the door folded back, and there sat Mr. Brown. Our peddler truck's driver!

"Mr. Brown! Now just what in tarnation are you doing here? I didn't know you drove a school bus." I felt so much better seeing someone I knew.

"Good morning, Little One. My truck is parked until next spring, so I thought I'd try driving this bus until then." The bus doors closed quietly behind me.

"You're the last one I'm picking up, so that means you'll be the first one off. You won't be on the bus very long either way. Why don't you sit in the seat behind me? Nobody else wants to sit close to the driver." Then Mr. Brown laughed, and it sounded like one of Mama's chickens cackling.

"Okay. I believe I will."

"When we start home, just before you get off the bus, I've got a few Tootsie Rolls I'll save for you. Just in case you have a rough first day." And he winked and grinned.

My day suddenly looked a lot more hopeful. Yep, this school year might work out pretty well.